TURNING POINT

Josh strode into Mary Taubin's office and dropped his book on the speech therapist's desk. "I'm kuh, kuh, kuh, quit . . . quitting," he said.

"Quitting?"

Josh nodded.

"I have something I want you to hear, Josh," Mary said, switching on her tape recorder. ". . . tuh, tuh, talking is tuh, tuh, tuh, terr . . . terrible for me," a girl's voice said. "I cuh, cuh, can't."

Mary stopped the recorder. "That was me, Josh. My stuttering was as bad as yours. Maybe worse. I know just how you feel. I wanted to quit, too. And I did quit for a year. It was the worst year of my life. That's why I won't let you quit, Josh."

She clicked on the tape recorder and Josh opened his book. He found the page. The words blurred through his tears. But he cleared his throat and began to read . . .

Bestsellers from SIGNET VISTA

Nobody's Brother

ANNE SNYDER
AND
LOUIS PELLETIER

A SIGNET VISTA BOOK

NEW AMERICAN LIBRARY

TIMES MIRROR

Publisher's Note

This novel is a work of fiction. Names, characters, places, and incidents are either the product of the author's imagination or are used fictitiously, and any resemblance to actual persons, living or dead, events, or locales is entirely coincidental.

Copyright © 1982 by Anne Snyder and Louis Pelletier

RL 4/IL 5+

SIGNET, SIGNET CLASSICS, MENTOR, PLUME, MERIDIAN AND NAL BOOKS are published by The New American Library, Inc., 1633 Broadway, New York, New York 10019

First Printing, August, 1982

1   2   3   4   5   6   7   8   9

PRINTED IN THE UNITED STATES OF AMERICA

It is with deep appreciation for the enthusiastic help and support of the entire staff at the Children's Speech and Hearing Center, Van Nuys, California, that the authors gratefully dedicate this book.

A.S.
L.P.

Chapter One

Josh should have known something awful was going to happen. The four of them hadn't had dinner together for almost as long as he could remember. Maybe a half dozen times in the three years since his mother married Bill.

And there they were pushing the food around on their plates, uncomfortably listening to his mother, waiting for the bomb, the disaster, whatever it was that had brought them to the seldom used dining room table.

His mother, Sandra, was smiling as she talked, being very civilized, including him in the grown-up dialogue. After all, he, Joshua, was sixteen, she was saying. He was old enough to realize the problem.

He looked at her almost objectively, as if she weren't his mother. She was so beautiful, so serene, so remote, her love so unobtainable, sometimes given generously, sometimes withheld for days on end as she tended her business in her posh office on Wilshire Boulevard. But he hated it when she sounded phony, such as speaking of "relating" to a problem instead of saying simply, "Let's try understanding it." Even his younger brother, Howie, agreed. Well, Howie was not really his brother, but was Bill's son, and therefore Josh's stepbrother. But he always thought of Howie as his real brother . . .

"Joshua . . ."

He was only half-listening, even though he was churning up inside, waiting for the bomb, the disaster.

And it was there, right out in front of them on the table. She hadn't really used the buzz word yet. What she was saying was that she and Bill had grown in dif-

1

ferent directions, whatever that meant, and now they were going to live apart.

Howie, who was eleven and knew a buzz word when one was called for, pronounced it.

"Divorce," Howie said.

Josh's mother laughed lightly. "Well, yes, that's what it is, actually." But then she went on quickly, saying it was all for the best, and it would be all right because Josh could see Howie from time to time, and for a while, of course, Howie would stay on, and live here till Bill got settled up at Skytop.

"I know this is a little out of the blue," his mother added, smiling.

Out of the blue! Josh's stomach knotted into a tight ball; his face got red; his lips moved. He wanted to speak; the words were down within him someplace, locked in. But now the suddenly bottomless pit of the future hit him full force. A few months and Howie would go. The whole world would blow up; his brother would go.

He looked at his mother, defiant in his struggle to speak. Yes, he wanted to say, Howie was *his brother* as much or more than blood could tie two people together.

He turned to Howie because Howie could almost always unlock the words for him, but Howie wouldn't look up from his plate after he said the buzz word. *Divorce*.

Carmela came in with the dessert on a tray. The moment of silence on her entrance, the set, angry faces of the boys, told her what she had been suspecting the last few weeks. She rested the tray on the sideboard and began taking off the plates.

"Dessert," Sandra said cheerily. And Josh felt for the first time ever that he'd like to clout his beautiful mother.

"Your favorite," she said, turning to Howie.

And it was Howie's favorite. Chocolate and pistachio ice cream frozen into animal forms. A glistening brown and green rabbit waited for him on the sideboard.

"I don't want any," Howie said, not looking up.

"Howie," Bill said gently.

2

Josh sucked in a huge breath. He felt his throat muscles tighten; his lips moved; then the words exploded. "He . . . he . . . he doesn't want the ruh . . . ruh . . . rabbit!"

Josh looked around the table, angrily taking large gulps of breath.

"Okay, Josh," Bill said quietly. "It's okay."

Sandra's jaw tightened a little. "Serve the dessert, Carmela."

Carmela took off the last plate. She spoke to herself softly in Spanish, looking in her mind's eye toward the little bedroom off the kitchen where the Virgin was enshrined over her bed, and called on the Blessed Lady to intercede, to bring peace to the family. She placed a frozen elephant on Bill's plate, a crouching cat for Josh, a chocolate poodle for Sandra, and then the brown and green rabbit for Howie.

Howie wouldn't look at the rabbit.

"Howie," Bill said, "Sandra went all the way to Gerson's in Beverly Hills . . ."

Howie lifted his chin, glared at his father. He took the plate with the frozen rabbit and threw it with all his fury at the dining room window, shattering the glass. He jumped up and ran out of the room.

No one spoke. Slowly, Josh got up from his chair and followed Howie out.

Carmela went to the hall closet to get a broom to sweep up the glass.

Bill looked ruefully at Sandra. "That scene didn't play the way we wrote it."

"It's all right," Sandra said. "They're kids, they'll get over it."

"I wonder . . ." Bill said tentatively.

"We agreed," Sandra said firmly.

He looked at her, tried to smile. "Yeah, but . . . I don't know. Do you think we could possibly . . ."

"No, we could not possibly," Sandra said.

Bill nodded.

Sandra began delicately scraping the chocolate off the creamy poodle. She could hear Josh going down the

3

long hall to the boys' bedroom. She could hear the door open and close.

Howie was sitting on the bench in front of the TV with the sound off watching the Monday night football. Josh sat down alongside him.

"I hate them," Howie said. "I hate him and I hate her. I hate both of them."

"Who's kicking the field goal?" Josh asked.

"Pleston."

"He'll make it."

"He'll miss," Howie said.

Pleston missed the field goal.

"I hate them," Howie said.

Josh rumpled Howie's hair, shook the boy's head gently, nodded to the TV. "You want to get something funny?"

"Nothing's funny," Howie said. He leaned his head against Josh's shoulder.

Josh felt a splat of wet on his hand. Howie never cried. Howie was tough. But Howie was crying.

There was a quick knock on the door, and Bill came into the room. He stopped just inside the door and took in the scene. Then he strode over and pulled Howie to the lower bunk, sat down so he'd be face to face with his son. He wiped the tears off Howie's face with his fingers. Pained, Josh watched. He knew how ashamed Howie was of crying.

"Hey, fella, come on, it won't be so bad," Bill said.

Howie stared belligerently at his father.

Bill put his hands on the boy's shoulders. "Look, Howie, I'm going to have to leave now for Skytop, but before you know it, we'll be together again."

Howie snuffled, turned his face away.

"I'll miss you, too, believe me," Bill said gently. "By the time the snow falls, I'll have a place all fixed up for us at Skytop. A real bachelor's pad for you and me. We'll make up for lost time. Just the two of us."

The tears began to roll down Howie's face again. Josh turned away, looked out the window.

"I'll call you . . . regular. And write. Long letters. Tell

4

you everything that's going on. It'll be practically the same as if I were here."

At the window, Josh heard Howie snuffle again, then Bill's voice: "Now, come on, give your old man a hug." There was a pause. "Howie . . . Howie? There, that's better. Goodbye, son."

Josh heard Bill go to the door, open it. "So long, Josh," Bill said.

When the door closed, Josh turned away from the window, went over to Howie, put his hand on the boy's arm. "How about *The Space Behind Space?*" It was a science fiction book they were reading together.

Howie nodded, averting his face, still not admitting the tears. He quickly took off his shirt, shoes, and trousers and climbed into the lower bunk while Josh got the book.

Howie turned his face to the wall. "Okay," he said.

Josh leaned against the end of the bunk. "Where were we?"

"Approaching the planet Voton," Howie mumbled.

Josh began reading.

Funny, when he read to Howie he never fumbled a word or hesitated as he sometimes did in class. He could sail right along reading to Howie, not waiting for the tricky sounds like "bou" in *bounce* or "buh" in *bottle*. It was okay reading to Howie.

". . . and there, shining out of the black void, a pinpoint of hope, of mystery, of perhaps a new race of beings, was the small speck of light that was Voton, a hundred thousand miles away . . ."

Josh read on. Howie drifted off into the limitless reaches of space, then slowly into sleep.

After a while Josh closed the book. He sat still looking down at his brother. Then he heard a garage door open just outside his window. Bill was loading his suitcases into his car. Sandra stood nearby. Bill put the last suitcase in. He kissed Sandra gently on the cheek. Tall, slender, her shining blond hair drifting softly around her face, she walked regally back toward the house.

Josh turned from the window, put the book back on

5

the shelf. After a moment he heard Bill's car start up and drive off.

He went back to the TV, turned it on again without the sound. He watched the small figures run, kick, pass. He sat there until the game was over at eleven, then he climbed up into his bunk.

He lay there quietly. He could hear Howie roll over and say something in his sleep. Josh knew he wouldn't be able to sleep. It was all going around in his head. The buzz word, *divorce*. Over and over. The final, definite, no-road-back word. *Divorce*. Over and over.

Chapter Two

His mood was as somber as the fog-shrouded morning. He ran swiftly down the canyon road, through the gray, graffiti-smeared tunnel under the highway and out onto the empty beach.

Six A.M. Nothing moved. Not even the crouching gulls facing the small, listless waves. Josh ran in the hard sand near the water, his new running shoes stamping ribbed patterns as he lifted his heels into the stride. The new shoes had been a gift from Bill when they talked of Josh making the cross-country team.

But now, sport and running were far from his mind. He ran because he had to, unaware that he was seeking release from tension, from the miserable scene at the dinner table the night before.

His rhythm steadied as if he were pacing himself for the cross-country trials that were coming up soon. Slap, slap, the new shoes against the sand. Don't think about last night. Don't think about you and Howie being apart. Think about good things. About running, about a tall, cool glass of water at the end of the run. Think about girls.

Hey, that was an idea. Girls. Girls, past and present. Not that there were many in either direction. After all, there was always his speech problem. The talk, the rapping problem. He couldn't handle it. He couldn't fire the smart lines back and forth like other guys. He let the girls do the talking. Vickie, last year. Hey, that Vickie. She said he was mysterious, a loner. Heavy stuff, very romantic.

He wheeled around at the breakwater and started back. Yeah, he was a loner. He couldn't mix with the

7

guys in the locker room, or wouldn't, fearing a slip that would lead to ridicule. Once, he did. He cringed inside remembering it, thinking of the time he wanted to be one of the guys saying, "Right on, man," just like they did. Only it came out, "Ruh . . . ruh . . . right . . . uh . . . uh . . . on . . . muh . . . muh . . . man," and they laughed at him. That was way back in the eighth grade, but he never forgot it.

Yeah, he was a loner, all right. Till Howie came. That changed everything.

Howie had been staying with his Aunt Clara in Wisconsin when Sandra and Bill first started dating. Then, when they got serious, Bill brought Howie home.

Three years ago. But almost like yesterday. Josh could see his mother and Bill standing in the doorway of his room. They were going off to Palm Springs to be married on the lawn of a very fancy house that faced the seventh green of the San Angelo Golf Course. And Bill was holding this eight-year-old kid by the hand and saying, "Josh, this is Howie."

And Sandra was saying, "Joshua, this is your brother."

And Josh saying, "I'm nuh . . . nuh . . . nuh . . . nobody's brother!"

And Bill and Sandra laughing and hugging both of them and having a crazy breakfast with ice cream and cake and then waving good-bye.

Josh and Howie watched the car go out of the driveway. Josh went back to his room and got his running shoes out of the closet. Howie stood in the doorway.

"How old are you?" Howie asked.

"Thirteen," Josh said.

"Where you going?"

"Running."

"Could I come?"

Josh shrugged. He didn't want an eight-year-old kid tagging along. It would look foolish.

"I can run pretty fast," Josh said.

Howie nodded.

Josh got up, ran in place, trying to look very authentic.

8

Howie was wearing big, klutzy sneakers, but he ran in place just like Josh.

Josh frowned. The kid was going to be a pest.

Carmela looked up from the dishes as Josh went out the kitchen door. She smiled to see Howie following. The boys were getting along, she thought.

Josh started out easily, aware that Howie was right behind him, but trying not to show it. They made an odd-looking pair, just as Josh had feared. Howie was a chunky, well-built kid with yellow hair down over his ears. Josh was dark, slim, handsome even then at thirteen.

Josh upped the pace a little. They were on the level approaching the long rise up into the canyon. He could hear the clump of Howie's heavy sneakers hitting the pavement.

They began to climb the hill. Josh couldn't help it; he had to show the kid how it was done. But Howie was right behind him, his small legs pounding to keep up with Josh's own long stride.

He glanced back. The dumb kid didn't know when he'd had enough. Ah, forget him, forget it, there was too much else to think about, too much else to get angry about.

His mother and Bill, that was enough for starters. Them getting married. Bill being his father. Creepy. That was really creepy. Not that Bill was bad or anything. He just wouldn't be like a real father. Josh couldn't remember his real father. He had an old snapshot someplace of himself perched on his father's shoulder, but that was all. His father cut out when Josh was two, and they never heard from him again. And there remained only that one snapshot of a tall, dark, good-looking guy.

Josh looked back. The stupid kid was only a few paces behind. Josh moved into high. The kid's legs pounded his klutzy sneakers into the pavement, but he still kept up.

The hill got steeper, up and up. Josh went over the top, panting. He stopped, looked back. Howie was a few yards behind, his hands on his knees, whoopsing his breakfast, ice cream, cake, and all.

Josh walked back slowly. Well, the kid had guts. He almost made it up the hill.

"You all right?" Josh asked.

Howie nodded, wiped his face with the back of his sleeve.

They walked back down the hill, not saying anything. Howie had to stop once more and unload the last of the breakfast.

Later that day, Carmela took them to the beach. Howie swam out so far Josh had to go in and bring him back. It looked like the crazy kid would try anything.

That night they tossed for bunks. Howie won and took the lower. In minutes he was asleep. Josh sat a long time looking at one of his sports magazines, but not really reading, thinking over and above the words on the page.

Then, suddenly, Bill and Sandra phoned to say that they were married and asked how he and Howie were getting along. Josh could hear music and laughter in the background. His mother sounded just a little giddy. She asked him to take good care of Howie, and he said he would.

He put down the phone and looked over at the sleeping Howie. For some reason he couldn't figure, Josh began crying and couldn't stop. He climbed into the upper bunk and lay down, cursing himself for behaving like a baby. But he still couldn't stop crying . . .

All that was three years ago, yet he remembered it all very vividly. Now, Josh eased his pace. He could make out his house as the sun began to break through the fog and warm his back.

Almost with surprise, he realized that this would be another of those ordinary, sunshiny California days.

He jogged the last quarter-mile to the house, then slowed to a walk. He was reluctant to go in, to face the problems awaiting him. He sat on the front step, shaking the sand out of his shoes, and then finally, he went inside the house.

Sandra was seated at the breakfast table. She looked

up from her newspaper as Josh entered. "Good morning," she said casually.

Josh nodded. "Where's Howie?"

"He left for school. He said something about an early assembly."

Carmela came in from the kitchen, set a glass of juice down at Josh's place. "Comé," she said in Spanish. "Eat." She turned to the sideboard. Josh could tell Carmela was upset by the stiff set of her shoulders, the way she plunked the plate of scrambled eggs before him. That told it all. Howie must have bolted out of the house without eating his own breakfast.

Josh wasn't very hungry either, but he dug into the eggs. He was in no mood to have Carmela rag at him for not eating.

Sandra finished her coffee, stood up. "I'm driving past the school. I'll drop you."

"I'm riding my bike," Josh said into his plate.

"Put it in the station wagon. I'll meet you in front."

Sandra was humming along with the car radio when Josh slid into the seat beside her. He slammed the door harder than necessary.

"Beautiful day for surfing," Sandra said. She smiled at him. "Why don't you and Howie go to the beach after school?"

"Not today," Josh mumbled. He looked across at her. He could almost hear her thinking: let's be bright and cheery, smooth it out, cover it up, pretend that what happened last night really wasn't important . . . only a slight shift of gears, nothing more. He watched as she steered the car expertly out of the driveway and into the tree-lined street.

"Mmm, everything smells so good today," Sandra said, rolling down her window.

Josh stared at her hands. Despite the long, manicured nails, blunted stylishly at their ends, her hands were strong, competent, and sure on the wheel.

She flicked him a look. "You okay?"

He shrugged. No, he was not okay, he thought. He

11

was terrible, awful. And so was Howie. But she was okay. She was always okay.

They drove on about a block, the radio music filling an obvious void. Abruptly, Sandra switched off the radio, pulled the car up at the curb.

She turned to him, put her hand on his shoulder. "Look, Josh, Bill and I . . . it was a mistake. You can understand that, can't you?"

He shook off her hand, looked at her bleakly.

"All right," she said edgily. "It's not easy. It's not easy for any of us. But it's nobody's fault, nothing I can do about it." She paused. "What do you expect me to do about it?"

Josh chose his words carefully. He spoke slowly. He didn't want to bungle it. "Howie. He can . . . live . . . with us. He . . . can . . . stay with us."

Their eyes locked. Sandra sighed impatiently. "You know he can't." She stopped, waiting for Josh to answer her. Then she went on. "Okay, I'll explain it again. Howie doesn't belong to us. He belongs to Bill. It wouldn't be right to keep him. Tell me, would that be fair to Bill?"

What's fair? thought Josh angrily. He and Howie were being split apart with nothing to say about it. Was that fair to Howie? To him?

He wanted to tell his mother what he was thinking. All the words were there welling up in his chest, his throat, pushing to come out. He tried to say them. His face contorted, grew red. He held his breath, felt a throbbing in his ears.

"If you have something to say, Joshua, then say it."

But he couldn't. He couldn't say it without stammering, stuttering, coming off like a blithering idiot.

"I'm waiting," Sandra said.

He clenched his fists, tried again. But the words were damned up. They were trapped someplace behind an unmovable barrier.

Suddenly, he slumped down in his seat. He felt drained. It was as if all the pent-up rage were seeping right out of his pores. He looked down at the floorboard.

"Go ahead. What is it you want to say?"

Josh rubbed his clammy hands on his knees. What was the use? There wasn't any use.

Irritated, Sandra turned the key in the ignition. "All right. Clam up. Cut me off as usual. End of discussion."

She started the car, jerked it into the traffic lane, and headed on down the hill.

Josh pulled his bike out of the station wagon, set it down, slammed the tailgate shut.

Standing at the signal across from the school, he waited for the light to change.

The high school was just off Sunset Boulevard at the foot of the canyon where the lushly mortgaged homes looked down on the Pacific Ocean. Josh pedaled across the boulevard on the green light, joining the morning crowd moving on toward the school.

Student cars were entering the parking lot, some Porsches, a few 280 Z's. There was even an occasional Mercedes, given, Josh knew, as a terrified tribute of love by some intimidated parent.

Because they lived only a mile up the canyon, he generally biked to school. Most times he was aware of the status symbols, the sports cars and the other subtle signals of student acceptance; he observed the little alligators on the left side of many guys' shirts, the Topsiders shoes, the right shade of body tan, the properly faded jeans. These things he unconsciously admitted as part of the school scene. But he had never been fully into the scene himself. He had friends; he played the required sports, but nobody yelled, "Hi, there's old Josh," or "Hi, Josh, how ya doin'?"

This morning, Josh was not aware of any of it. There was still so much scrambling around in his head. Yesterday he had a family. Not a solid family, not a true blue family: mom, pop, two related kids, Disneyland, ski trips, a summer place at the lake, but a family nevertheless. Today, nothing. That was all he could think of. The big nothing, all down the road.

He sat in English class, his chin on the palm of his hand, looking out the window up into the hills. Not far up there, hidden by the trees, was the lovely Spanish-

13

style house his mother had bought when her business suddenly prospered ten years ago, and when Carmela had come up from Ensenada to take care of him.

"Taylor?"

Miss Deemers, the English teacher, used last names, and Josh was not immediately aware that he was being called on. Okay, he was Taylor, but his mother's name was now Robinson. And who knew what new name she'd have next time.

"Taylor, could you tell us the difference between metaphor and simile?"

Josh turned toward Miss Deemers. At once he felt a pounding, quickening of pulse. He knew he wouldn't be able to say the word, *metaphor*. He'd block on it for sure.

He took deep breaths while Miss Deemers waited. He'd been able to get through most classes by adroit switches to less threatening words, but now he'd have to say this one.

The long pause had caused several heads to turn in his direction.

"Meh ... meh ... meh ..."

The boy behind him gave Josh a small prod with his toe. A couple of nearby girls began to giggle.

Josh knew he wasn't going to be able to make it this time. For years he had buried the problem in a maze of clever word substitutions, and with practice, he had gotten quite good at it. At home it wasn't as easy. His mother was baffled and embarrassed when he was blocked and struggling for expression. And sometimes he'd just clam up, knowing he was trapped by a word or a phrase. She misread the clamming up, thinking of it as an act of defiance, hating the silent, frightened look he'd get while his whole body seemed to join in the struggle to make the sound come out.

Abruptly, the bell rang. Josh slumped back in his seat sweating profusely, gulping large breaths of air.

Miss Deemers smiled. "We'll return to the metaphors tomorrow. Put all book reports in the basket, please."

The class filed out, dropping their papers into the basket on Miss Deemers' desk.

14

Josh didn't move. His pulse was still racing with nameless fear. They'd find him out some day, laugh at him, giggle at him, drop him to a low-comedy level, the butt of the joke. He'd be different, unacceptable, even wearing the alligator on his shirt, even having his jeans just the right faded blue.

He felt, rather than saw, Miss Deemers' eyes on him. He got up, put his book report in the basket. The teacher smiled up at him. "I think you could use some help," she said.

Josh looked at her questioningly. He was doing all right in English. History was where he was weakest.

"Taylor, I've made an appointment for you with Miss Taubin."

"Tuh ... Tuh ... Tuh ... Taubin?"

"The speech therapist."

It was as if she had struck him. He was too stunned to answer.

Deemers went on, "I've been talking to Miss Taubin about you, Taylor. She's agreed to see you tomorrow."

"I ... don't ... need ... any help," Josh said slowly.

"Let's see what Miss Taubin thinks." She handed him a piece of paper. "You'll find the time and place on the appointment slip."

"Buh ... buh ... buh ... but ... I duh ... duh ... duh ... don't ..."

Deemers interrupted him. "Miss Taubin will see you tomorrow, Taylor," she said gently.

Josh turned and bolted out of the room.

Chapter Three

The elementary school was just a few blocks from the high school. Josh usually picked Howie up in the afternoon and they biked home together.

Josh put his bike in the rack at the entrance to the playground. There was some sort of hassle going on in one corner of the playground near the fence, a ring of boys yelling with two unseen fighters in the middle.

Josh sighed. One of the fighters had to be Howie.

It *was* Howie.

"All right, all right!" Josh yelled. "Buh . . . buh . . . break it up! Come on, you guh . . . guh . . . guys, break it up!"

Josh waded into the middle of the ring and grabbed Howie. Some kids grabbed the other fighter.

"Let 'em finish!" a skinny kid yelled.

Josh grabbed the skinny kid by the back of the collar. "You want to fuh . . . fuh . . . fuh . . . finish it?" he asked angrily.

"Not me," the kid said. He pointed to Howie. "He called him a horse's butt, not me."

"He *is* a horse's butt," Howie said.

The other fighter struggled to resume, but Josh took hold of Howie's shirt and propelled him out of the crowd toward the bike rack.

"Let go," Howie said.

Josh let go.

"Why do you always pick on him?" Josh asked. "He's bigger than you."

"He's the biggest." Howie said.

"So why him?"

"He's a horse's butt, that's why. A great big horse's butt."

16

Josh put his arm around Howie's shoulder. "Okay. But some day I'm going to be late and he's going to wipe up the floor with you."

Howie looked up and smiled. "So don't be late."

Josh laughed.

Howie clung to the back of Josh's belt, proud that everybody could see this fantastic brother who called for him almost every day.

They soon were pedalling across the boulevard on the light and started up the canyon toward home. Howie rode up ahead as always. Josh watched him with an inward smile. Howie would be handsome some day, but now, at eleven, he was the usual California kid with scorched blond hair, gray-blue eyes, unwanted freckles on the nose, and, of course, an alligator over the left side of his shirt.

Josh thought he couldn't remember a time that he didn't feel that Howie was the greatest kid ever, but there had been a time. That first day when Bill brought him to their house.

Bill, his stepfather.

Josh liked Bill but he never could connect him with the word, *father*. Bill was his mother's husband. Or just Bill, a casual friend around the house.

When Sandra was dating Bill it was kind of exciting for Josh. Bill had played pro football for one season, so he took Josh to some games and even brought him back to the locker room to meet the players. Josh was only thirteen at the time but he was aware that this was some kind of grown-up strategy, a softening-up process so he'd like Bill when he and Sandra got married.

Not that he didn't like Bill, but it was awful crafty the way they had maneuvered him. Okay, Bill was fun. He was actually three years younger than Sandra, well built, nice looking. After he quit football he got a cinch job as a stockbroker, "account executive" they called him. A lot of rich men who had watched Bill in pro football threw their accounts his way. Bill didn't have to work very hard, so he and Sandra could go off on wonderful trips to Aspen and Acapulco and Palm Springs and long cruises on customers' yachts, stuff like that.

17

While they were only dating Josh could take it, and Carmela would keep telling him that everything was going to be fine, especially since he was going to have a brother, Bill's eight-year-old son who was then staying with Bill's sister.

Then one day Sandra announced that she and Bill had set a date for the wedding. Even though he knew it was coming, it still hit Josh hard. He went up to his room, locked the door, and flopped on his bunk. He didn't know why he was bummed out. He'd never had a father; all he had was a snapshot. And now Sandra was saying he'd have a father and a brother, and still, there he was in the pits.

Howie got off his bike to push it up the last very steep part of the hill before their own driveway.

"Josh?"

"Yeah."

"Will I be here for Christmas?"

Josh shrugged. "Who knows?"

"Can you come see me at Skytop?"

"I guess so. Maybe. I don't know," Josh said.

They pushed their bikes up the hill, thinking ahead. Skytop was the big ski and summer resort three hundred miles north of the city. It had grown so large and popular that Bill's brokerage firm was getting ready to open an office there and Bill was going to be the manager.

"Josh?"

"Yeah."

Howie stopped, looked up at Josh, then shook his head. "Nothing."

"Nothing what?"

Howie shrugged. "Just nothing, that's all."

"Okay," Josh sighed. "I know what you mean."

Howie pushed the bike up into the driveway.

Josh stopped, watched Howie work the bike into the rack they'd built in the side yard. The way Howie moved the bike, the rough swinging way he handled it suddenly unlocked a memory for Josh. Way back. A couple of weeks after Howie had come to live with them. They had worked out a kind of truce, fragile but hold-

18

ing. Then one day Sandra came to him with a worried frown. It was Carmela's day off, and she and Bill had been invited to a fabulous party. Would Josh babysit Howie?

Josh smiled to himself. He could heard Howie's voice, even now, hear just the way he said it.

"You're sitting me?" said Howie with wide-eyed incredulity.

"Yeah," said Josh.

"Where's Carmela?"

"Day off."

"You can't sit me; you're only thirteen."

"So?"

"They paying you?"

"Yeah," Josh said. "Why?"

"How much?"

"Look, you do your homework, never mind how much."

"I did my homework."

"When?"

"I didn't have any."

"Well, go play your computer game."

"I already played it."

"Well, go look at TV."

"What's on?"

"How do I know?"

"You're the sitter," Howie said.

Josh got out the *TV Guide*. "A monster flick, *The Blood of the Werewolf*, okay?"

Howie didn't answer. He couldn't admit to his new brother that he wasn't really into horror movies.

"Hey," Howie said, "you don't have to turn out the lights."

"Makes it scarier," Josh said.

The movie was a super horror, with fangs dripping blood and little kids running in terror from the werewolf. When it was over and Josh turned on the lights Howie's face was pale and he was sitting very still.

"Okay," Josh said, "time for bed. Go on, I'll lock up."

"I'll wait for you," Howie said softly.

Josh looked at the pale, still face. "Hey . . . you scared?"

Howie said no with a shake of his head, but the rest of him plainly said yes.

Josh felt a sudden rush of tenderness. "Nothing to be scared of."

Howie nodded again, not speaking.

"Okay," said Josh. "You help me lock up."

Howie followed Josh closely as Josh checked the locks. When Sandra's cat, Suzy, dropped down from the kitchen cabinet and upset a bowl of sugar, Howie grabbed Josh and wouldn't let go.

Josh put his arm around Howie's shoulder. "It's only Suzy," Josh said.

They locked the house and went to their bedroom.

Howie didn't brush his teeth or set out his clothes for school, or anything. He just crawled in his bunk and pulled up the covers.

Josh sat at the edge of the bunk.

"You okay?" he asked.

Howie nodded uncertainly.

"Well, I guess we'd better get some sleep," Josh said.

"Don't turn out the light."

"You want to stay up all night?"

"You could read to me. When I couldn't sleep, my Aunt Clara used to read to me."

Josh went to Howie's book shelf.

"I like space," Howie said.

Josh picked out *Voyage to Eternity*.

He sat at the foot of the bed, began to read. "One million light years from earth in a galaxy where time and space were one . . ."

Josh read on and as he read he became aware of something incredible, unbelievable. Not the galaxy, not the billions of stars, but he, Joshua, was reading to his brother, Howie, and not stumbling on a single word. And looking back he realized that he had been talking to Howie all evening and hadn't stumbled once.

Suddenly the impossible seemed possible. He could speak fluently. Okay, just to one person, just to one scared eight-year-old kid. But if he could do this . . .

Howie was asleep. Josh closed the book softly. Yeah, anything was possible.

The note from Miss Taubin lay on Sandra's desk in the den. She read it and frowned with irritation. Then she quickly corrected the frown. Frowning was out. Frowning made wrinkles and a woman competing in business didn't need an extra disadvantage. A man could have a hide like an elephant, but a woman in the fashion field fought the battle with her face. Serenity, beauty, poise; these were valuable weapons. Sandra had them all. Frowning was out.

She read the note again and sighed heavily. An occasional sigh was not too damaging.

"Joshua . . ." she called.

Josh was studying in the living room with Howie. The TV was on without the sound so they could watch the basketball game over Josh's history book and Howie's math homework.

"Joshua!"

He got up reluctantly from the basketball game and went down the hall to the den. His mother handed him Miss Taubin's note.

"Will you read this, please?"

Josh read the note.

"Why does this Miss Taubin think you have a speech problem?"

Josh shrugged, looked down at the floor.

"You don't really have a speech problem, do you, Joshua?"

He shook his head negatively.

"Then why does Miss Taubin think it would be constructive if I would go to see her on Monday?"

"She . . . she just wants to . . ." He fought for the word. ". . . to talk to you, I guess."

Sandra looked at him impassively, waiting.

"That's . . . that's what they pay her for, I guess," he said lamely.

"Joshua . . ."

He looked up at her finally.

"If you concentrate, really concentrate, there is no problem. Right?"

He nodded. Of course there wasn't any problem. And if there were, even a little one, he wasn't going to embarrass her with it, make her sit down with Miss Taubin and listen to a lot of therapy talk. No way.

He used to feel awful when he embarrassed his mother, when he couldn't help himself. Like at the cocktail parties she'd give, or anytime when she'd introduce him and some guy would always ask if he played football and if he liked the Rams and he'd just shake his head and clam up, and his mother would jump in with a laugh and say he was shy and tell him to go out and play. But he didn't embarrass her anymore, fumbling words like an idiot. No way would he ever do that again.

"Joshua . . ." She was smiling now, and suddenly he was bathed in the glory of the smile. "I've got a showing in Denver on Monday. "Do you think . . ."

"Sure, I . . . I'll tell her. Don't worry, Mom."

She put her hands on his shoulder and kissed his cheek. "You're okay, Joshua." She took the history book out of his hand, opened it. "You know, I was good in history. I'll bet you are too."

"I . . . I stink in history," Josh said.

They laughed together. She held him close for a moment and he could smell the wonderful perfume she wore and he loved her very much. He wasn't going to stumble over his words anymore, or ever embarrass her as long as he lived.

Chapter Four

Josh sat in the empty bleachers, the sun feeling good on his face, and watched the sprinters run their laps. This was where he often came when he wanted to be alone during lunchtime.

Faint girlish laughter carried up to the bleachers. He squinted over toward the side of the field. The Phys Ed teacher was supervising freshman calisthenics. Generally, Josh enjoyed the spectacle of the girls, in their shorts and T-shirts, going through their paces, especially the running in place. But today he couldn't keep his mind on what was going on down there.

As he bit into his sandwich, a shot of anxiety stabbed the pit of his stomach. The appointment with the speech therapist. Fifth period. Right after lunch. No way out. He'd have to show.

With trembling fingers, he opened his milk carton, took a swallow. His stomach grumbled. He could report to the nurse. Cry bellyache. Get excused. Go home.

Still, why prolong the agony? Make the interview, get it over with. He'd play it right, get Deemers off his back. He'd be home safe. It would be easy, a piece of cake. He'd let the therapist do all the talking. It was really amazing how much you could let the other guy speak for you. People loved hearing themselves talk, took the words right out of your mouth. And Josh had always been glad to let them.

He looked at his watch. Nothing to be nervous about, he told himself. He had the whole meeting planned out, had practiced in his head almost all night long. He went over it again now: His name. Joshua Taylor . . . no, Josh Taylor . . . no, only Josh. Then the therapist would look down at Miss Deemers' report and say, "Joshua Taylor, right?" And all Josh would have to do was nod.

As for the rest of it, he'd say only the words he was sure of, the phrases on which he never stumbled. "No problem," he'd say at the end of the interview.

"No problem," the therapist would write on the report. And that would be that. No problem.

Josh put down his milk carton, reached for his sandwich, changed his mind. He wasn't very hungry. And the little bit of sandwich he'd already eaten seemed to be stuck right under his Adam's apple.

The small name plate on the half-open door read MARY TAUBIN. Josh sighed deeply, reached out to knock. Suddenly the door swung inward, and he was looking down, eyeball to eyeball, at a young face all but lost in a mass of tousled, crimped red hair.

"Come on in," the girl said.

Josh looked over her head for the therapist. There was no one else in the room. Waving him to come along, the girl crossed the room and flopped into an upholstered chair in front of the desk. She put her feet up on a low-slung coffee table littered with books, cassettes, papers. She gestured toward the other chair opposite the table, and Josh sat down.

He looked at her. She had a plain but pleasant face, and, like most student assistants, he thought, she had a certain proprietary air about the office she worked in.

"Mary Taubin," said the girl.

"Huh?" Josh said.

She laughed, pointed to herself. "Me, Mary Taubin." Then she pointed at him and grinned, "You, Joshua Taylor."

Josh couldn't help laughing. Surprise number one. This little, skinny kid was the speech therapist! He relaxed, leaned back in his chair. This was going to be easier than he thought. A breeze.

"Okay, down to business," Mary said. "Do you know why you're here?"

Josh shrugged. He had anticipated this question, was

24

ready for it. Slowly, carefully, he said, "Miss Deemers. She thinks I need help."

"Do you?"

Josh smiled. "No."

Mary smiled back. "Fine," she said.

Surprise number two. He hadn't counted on the opposition buckling under this quickly. He felt foolish for having worried about it. As if he'd been ready to use a sledge hammer to kill an ant. He moved forward in his chair, almost getting ready to leave.

Then surprise number three hit him right between the eyes. Mary tossed a book in his lap. "Read," she said. He looked at her. "Any place. Just read aloud. Any old paragraph."

He took the book in his hands, flipped through it, stalling for time.

"Go ahead," Mary said.

He took a deep breath. Take it easy, he told himself. Pretend you're reading to Howie. He began: "'. . . So Jim went to work and told me the whole thing right through . . .'" He stopped. Could he get over the next word? He started again. "'. . . right through cuh . . . cuh . . . cuh . . .'" He began to perspire; he could feel the blood rise to his face. "'. . . cuh . . . cuh . . . cuh . . .'" The word is *considerably*, his head told him. You can say it. *Considerably*. Say it! But his mouth couldn't form the word. He clutched the book tighter, went back a few words. "'. . . the whole thing right through cuh . . . cuh . . . cuh . . . cuh . . .'" And then the word shot out of his mouth like an explosion. "'Considerably!'" he shouted.

The book fell from his hands. He bent over, picked it up, dropped it again.

"Leave it there," Mary said gently. "It's okay."

She watched him carefully as he folded his arms, unfolded them, let them drop in his lap. He shifted back in his seat, clutched the arms of the chair. He avoided her steady gaze, found a far corner of the room to focus on. A plant was hung in a wicker basket, its leaves drooping over the sides.

25

Now Mary flipped on a tape recorder. Josh's head snapped back at the sound.

"Tell me when it's most difficult for you to speak," Mary said.

Josh looked back at the corner of the room. The plant swayed with a breeze from the open window.

"Tell me, Josh."

He pressed his lips tightly shut, a muscle twitched in his cheek.

"Okay, when's it easiest?"

He remained silent, kept his eyes on the plant.

"Answer me, Josh." He looked at her fiercely. "Oh, the tape recorder," she said. Leaning over, flipping it off, she said, "Lots of people get self-conscious when they're being taped. Now. Is it better at school or at home?"

Still, Josh kept his silence. She had tricked him. He fell for it once, he wouldn't again. He'd keep his mouth shut. She'd get nothing more from him.

"What about reciting in class? How do you manage?"

Unperturbed, she met his angry stare. "Are there certain situations, circumstances that are worse than others?"

Josh answered in his head. Yeah, like right now! Like what you're trying to do to me! Trip me up, corner me! Well, just try! Go ahead! See how far you get!

The two continued to look into each other's eyes; Josh, with rage; Mary, with compassion. Finally, Josh shuffled his feet, looked down at the floor.

"I'm trying to help you."

"Duh . . . duh . . . don't need any!"

"We'll start with two sessions a week and see how it goes," Mary said quietly.

"Won't cuh . . . cuh . . . cuh . . . come!"

"Consider it part of your education. No big deal."

Josh shook his head.

Mary sighed softly. "You don't have a choice."

"Cuh . . . cuh . . . cuh . . . can't . . ." he began. He gulped air. "No time!" he blurted out.

Mary shuffled some papers on the table, picked one up. "I see you have study period right after lunch. We'll schedule you for that time Tuesdays and Thursdays."

She smiled, stood up. "No problem," she said firmly.

Josh disliked him the minute his mother's new male friend walked in the room. Carmela said, "La señora comes momento," and left for the kitchen.

Josh and Howie were watching TV in the living room when the guy came in. He was tall and okay looking but with a phony smile under a heavy dark brown mustache. Josh didn't know who the guy was trying to impress with his Gucci loafers and the four-hundred-dollar sport coat and the French cuffs with the lion-headed solid-gold cufflinks. All Josh knew was that he disliked the guy instantly.

And he wasn't liking his mother too much either at this awkward moment. Here it was only a week since Bill had left and she was already dating. And the guy was obviously younger than she was.

"Hi," the man said.

"Hi," Josh said. Howie didn't even turn around.

The man went straight across the room to the bar and began mixing himself a drink. Just like he owned the place.

Josh turned back to the TV. It was a cop show with cars crashing and guns blazing and bosomy girls getting hands clapped over their mouths so they wouldn't scream. Josh wasn't really into it but, like Howie, he was stalling until it was time to get down to their homework.

The guy came over with a Scotch in his hand and sat down in the big chair to look at the TV. One of the bosomy girls was struggling with one of the baddies and the camera was favoring the very tight pair of jeans she was wearing.

"I really go for those jeans," the guy said grinning over at Josh.

Josh didn't return the grin. He could feel Howie tense up when the guy spoke. You certainly couldn't blame Howie either. He'd been missing Bill, Josh knew, and here was some flashy new creep trying to move in.

Sandra came floating into the room. She was wearing a new dinner dress and an aura of heady perfume. She held out both hands, but the creep didn't even jump up.

He held out his left hand and said, "Heyyy," lazily, looking her over with appreciation.

"Jack, you haven't met the boys," she said. "This is my son, Joshua, and my stepson, Howie."

"Hi," the boys perfunctorily repeated.

As if she needed to explain, Sandra went on. "Mr. Bender is sales representative for Fairfield Sportswear. We're showing his line in San Francisco next week."

Josh wanted to say something scathing like, "That's peachy dandy," but he was churning inside and he knew he'd blow it with a "puh . . . puh," on the *peachy*, so he just kept quiet.

Jack looked at his watch. "We'd better get moving, huh, Sandy?"

Sandra nodded and picked up the delicate piece of mink that topped her perfect costume.

Brief goodnights were exchanged, and Sandra said that Carmela had a special treat for them if they could struggle through their homework. Then she was gone.

When she got to the door Josh had a funny feeling that all of this had happened many times before. Only it had been his mother and Bill the other times. They hardly ever ate at home. There was always some party or some long weekend or a quick hop to Palm Springs. But always his mother at the door, looking beautiful and saying Carmela had a treat for them, Carmela would take care of them.

Howie stood up to look out the living room window as Jack's car, an old dark green Bentley, went down the driveway. He had seen a car like this in one of Josh's sports magazines, but he didn't know that it was the "in" car that season. He just knew Jack Bender was a total creep, and it made him feel sick inside.

He turned from the window. "Hey, I really go for those jeans," he said acidly, mimicking Jack Bender.

Josh smiled wearily.

"A creep," Howie said.

Josh nodded.

"What does she want with a creep?"

"You heard her," Josh said. "Business."

"Business," Howie echoed scornfully.

28

"Well, maybe it *is* business," Josh said.

"Yeah," said Howie, doubly scornful.

"Look," Josh said, "she can go out with anybody she wants. It doesn't have to be business."

"Yeah," Howie said.

"Well, yeah what?"

"Just yeah, she can go out with anybody she wants."

Josh turned off the TV. "All right," he said angrily, "you've got homework, get going."

"I'll do it in the morning."

"Now!" Inside, Josh's heart was pounding. What a thing to do. To yell at Howie. For what?

"Howie . . ."

"Okay," Howie said softly. He got up from the bench in front of the TV and walked slowly to the entry hall.

Josh wanted to call him back, say forget the homework, let's go out and run and not stop until it gets dark. But he didn't say anything. He let Howie go.

He sat in front of the dead TV, looking at nothing. She could have waited a little while. Or had she been seeing this creep before? No. No, it was business. Of course it was. Josh knew only vaguely what his mother did. Put on fashion shows, something like that. He had been taken to one when he was a kid, six or seven. It was in this hotel and there were all these girls walking up and down the runway showing off clothes, and Josh sat at a table with Carmela, and he had knocked a pitcher of water over, and that was the last fashion show he could remember.

He kept staring at the blank TV. His chin cupped in the palm of his hands, he thought about Jack Bender. It had to be business, it just had to. Anything else would be too much for him to handle.

Chapter Five

They were warming up on the infield grass, bending, stretching, running in place, eying each other cautiously, competitively. Josh had a lot of space around him as he did swinging bends to touch his toes. The others, most of them, worked out in small groups, kidding each other, faking a relaxed attitude before the run.

As Josh bent to his toes, he could see a particular girl sitting in the stands with some of her friends. They often gathered there after school, sipping Cokes, trading gossip, watching the young muscles on the infield grass.

Josh said her name to himself. Lisa Schiller. She sat next to him in American history and they smiled occasionally and said hi. Once she borrowed his notes on the Missouri Compromise. He often fantasized a date with Lisa, but he didn't want to risk a failure, an evening of bloopers with him duh . . . duh . . . duhing all over the place. Maybe some day he'd risk it, but right now wasn't the time. But she sure looked exciting sitting there sipping Coke, laughing with that marvelous way she had of throwing her head back and letting it go so that everyone around her had to join in. Terrific female, Lisa Schiller.

The whistle blew and they all gathered around the coach to hear what they already knew, that this would be a ten-kilometer run and would count on the point scores that determined who would be on the squad next spring. There would be twelve runners on the squad by a process of elimination, the twelve highest point scorers in this run and the next one just before mid-term exams. There were thirty-five hopefuls gathered around the coach as he went over the route they had to run.

Josh knew the route so well he could have travelled it in the dark. He had worked it over, stopwatch in hand, beating his own time each of the last three tries. He had set his pace to match the hills and level stretches. He was ready. But so were Eddie Lenz and Rick Meers and the black kid, Ronnie something-or-other. They were ready too. Okay, okay, let's go.

The starting gun popped and they swarmed out of the gate and down the hill that lead to the beach highway. The coach watched them go with a smile of satisfaction. He was going to have a pretty good squad next spring.

The first leg of the run was along the service road that bordered the beach. The gung-ho runners who were going to burn it out on the first hill were up front striding confidently. Josh was in the last ten, taking it easy, pacing himself carefully. It was hard to tell who was here in the back out of necessity and who was doing it the way he was.

The first hill was the sharp, steep rise from the beach. The front runners dug in confidently, wanting to keep the lead. But it was a mean hill. The pounding rubber soles hit into the pavement, but the hill seemed to be tilting higher as the runners panted toward the top.

Josh hit the summit breathing steadily. He glanced at Eddie Lenz, a smart runner. Eddie came over the top easily. So did Ronnie, the black, and Rick Meers. They were all playing it very cagey, and the front runners were beginning to ease back into the pack.

The level stretch along Rivera Boulevard was almost a third of the run. Now the smart ones were moving up, Josh among them. He couldn't avoid running alongside Eddie Lenz, and he could almost feel the hatred between them. It had been that way since ninth grade when Eddie made fun of Josh who was trying to say, "Sure, man," but it came out, "Sh . . . sh . . . sh . . . sure, man," and Josh had taken a swing at him. The fierce and bloody fight lasted for three minutes till they were separated. Neither one of them had ever forgotten.

Josh now began to pick up his pace a little, lifting his heels easily, moving up. He felt strong, confident. He passed other runners, hearing them breathing heavily.

31

The pack began to string out into fours, threes, twos, then singles. Ronnie was in tenth place now, Josh a few paces behind him, Eddie alongside Josh.

They turned around at Rivera and Fourth to go back the way they had come. This was business, the last half of the run. Now the twelve, whoever they would be, would have to make their moves.

Josh pressed ahead; Eddie Lenz kept at his side. They passed several runners. Josh wanted to move out, leave Eddie behind, but he knew it would be wrong. Eddie grinned at him, knowing what Josh knew. There was still the beach and the last climb back to the school.

Now they were pounding along the beach service road. Josh was in the first twelve. If he could only hold it.

The school cop held back the traffic across the beach highway. They hit the last hill. Eddie Lenz, like a terrier, was alongside. He was a runner, and he didn't even gasp for breath as he said, "Suh . . . suh . . . sure, man," and laughed and moved ahead.

That louse! That stinking, rotten louse! Josh opened his mouth and gulped large breaths of air. As he moved up, Eddie's elbow caught him in the chest, but he didn't even feel it. He passed Eddie Lenz. He dug into the hill, fought the hill, moved up past Rick, past Ronnie, then past Eddie Lenz and through the gate, number two. He stumbled onto the grass and flopped down gasping, but with joy.

The coach stood over him smiling. "Nice run," he said, looking at his stopwatch.

Elated, Josh grinned back at him.

Josh felt good all the way home. For the moment he forgot his problems, the hidden anxieties. Instead he looked down the road in his mind, and it was spring, and he was traveling with the squad to the interschool meet in San Jose. He was in the bus with the squad, and they were all laughing at something funny that he, Josh, had said, some fantastic punch line, and they were saying, "Sure, man, that Josh is something else."

He told Carmela first, hedging his bets a little in case he didn't make it on the next run. But Carmela only heard the good part, and she said she knew he would win because she had asked the Blessed Lady to intercede.

Josh laughed. "Thanks, Carmela."

She looked at him seriously. "Next Sunday you come to Mass with me. You tell our Lady, grácias."

Josh smiled, shook his head. "No dice, Carmela."

For years she had been trying to lure him into the Church, and once or twice he had gone to please her. It wasn't bad, but it didn't quite measure up to a good early morning run.

"Where's Mom?" he asked Carmela.

He wanted to tell his mother more than anyone, even Howie. His mother was always talking about how he ought to get himself involved, participate. She'd like this. He'd travel with the squad; maybe there would be a picture in the local paper. He could just hear her saying to some friend, "Oh yes, my Josh is very much into cross-country." He smiled to himself. He had never been "into" much of anything, but now this was something he could offer her.

"Where is she, Carmela?"

Carmela nodded toward the back of the house. "She gets dressed now."

Josh ran down the hall, knocked at his mother's door. She called, "Yes?"

"It's me, Mom. Something I've got to tuh . . . tuh . . . tell you. Im . . . important."

"I'll be out in a minute, Joshua."

"Okay."

He went into his room feeling very high. Bouncy, kind of. He pulled a record at random, put it on the turntable. It was an old Jackson Browne, beautiful beat. He stood looking down at the spinning disc, tapping his foot, softly slapping his side.

He heard the blast of a car horn. He looked out the window onto the driveway. Jack Bender's green Bentley had come to a stop. The horn sounded again, loud and demanding, arrogant. Josh's jaw set. The guy couldn't even come up and ring the bell; he had to blow his lousy horn.

A short wait and the horn blew again.

Sandra came running out of her bedroom, slipping things into her purse. She stopped at Josh's door, smiling, flushed with excitement.

"What is it, Josh, what did you want to tell me?"

"Nothing," Josh said.

"You said it was important."

"It'll keep."

"All right." She kissed him hastily. "I'll be home late, darling. Jack and I are going to this thing in Malibu. Lots of big movie people." She laughed. "I'll bring you a souvenir, a lock of Paul Newman's hair."

"Thanks, Mom."

"Be good, now. And give Howie a kiss for me."

Josh didn't look up at her. He didn't want to see the joy and excitement in her face.

Then she was gone. He watched Jack Bender give her a laughing, possessive hug, watched her get in the Bentley, watched it ease out of the driveway and down the hill.

He grabbed the record off the spinning player and smashed it against the side of the bed. Then he took out a handful of records and smashed them all, one by one, slowly, deliberately, fiercely, till his eyes blurred. Then he took the last one and broke it across his knee.

Carmela stood in the doorway looking at the mess of broken records. She came in the room and put her arms around him and held him close and said soft, soothing words to him in Spanish.

With a worried frown, Josh walked toward the speech therapy room. There was no way to refuse to go to Miss Taubin's speech therapy sessions without making waves at school. And there was no way to get Sandra to sign the permission slip excusing him from study period without making waves at home. So he had simply faked Sandra's signature on the permission slip. It made no difference really, Josh reasoned; this time he'd be on guard, concentrate, think about every word he uttered

34

before he said it. He'd show the therapist he didn't need her and that would be the end of it.

The door to Mary Taubin's room was open. Josh went in and looked around. For a moment he thought there was no one there.

"Up here," Mary called. She was standing on a tall stool watering the hanging plant in the corner. "Be right with you."

She finished watering, turned to face him. "Here," she said, holding the spouted can out to him. "Set it down someplace, will you?"

Josh put the watering can on the bookcase while Mary sprang to the floor. She ran her hands down the sides of her skirt to dry them. Then she sat down in a corner of the sofa, tucked her feet under her, patted a place beside her. "Sit," she said.

Josh took the chair opposite the table, where he had sat last time. He sat stiffly at the edge of the seat and looked at her. She rested an elbow on the back of the sofa, twirled a lock of her springy hair, smiled at him.

He nodded guardedly. This would not be a repeat of the last interview, he thought. He wouldn't be taken in by her phony casual act. He wouldn't say anything, talk into any tape recorder, nothing. Maybe he was required to come to her crummy session, give her the hour. But that's all she'd get from him. Just the time.

Mary leaned over the table, picked up an orange-colored paperback book, tossed it toward him.

"You'll find lots of information about speech disorders in there."

He tensed. Would she ask him to read aloud from the book? Well, he was ready for her this time. Defiantly, he put the book down on the table.

But Mary seemed not to notice. "Everyone knows what stuttering is," she said. "Everybody trips over a word once in a while, luh . . . luh . . . luh . . . like this, but there are different degrees of stuttering. And with some people—for different reasons—it gets to be a problem."

No problem, I've got no problem, Josh countered angrily inside his head. But he nodded again. Let her go

35

on. Let her talk; let her do all the talking. He looked down at the floor.

"When a person stammers, is disfluent, it's inconvenient, sometimes embarrassing . . ."

I know all that. Tell me something new, he thought bitterly.

". . . But it can be a lot more serious than that. It can sometimes influence a person's whole life. Take someone who wants to be a teacher, but can't lecture. Or a person who'd like to be an attorney, but couldn't plead a case. Hundreds, maybe thousands, have been forced to change the whole direction of their lives." She paused, then said quietly. "I know someone who has a true calling, but it's impossible for him to give a sermon. He's in the mail order business. He hates it."

Josh looked up at her. He'd never thought too much about that. About how it was for older people who stuttered. But he hardly ever heard anyone stutter except for those weird comics in old movies who did it just to get a laugh.

Mary got up, went to her desk, and poured herself a glass of water from a carafe.

Josh considered: Where were all the stuttering people? And what was she trying to tell him? That he'd still be stuttering years from now? No, she was just trying to scare him; that was it. He was already good at avoiding certain tough words; he'd get better at it. By the time he was grown, he'd be an expert. Or maybe would grow out of the whole thing.

Mary perched on the edge of the desk, water glass in hand. "Of course, there are the closet stutterers. We'll never know how many hide their defect, get around it one way or another."

So they did get away with it! Josh entertained the thought smugly. Okay, it was tough, but it could be done. She had just admitted that, hadn't she?

Mary finished the water and set down the glass. Then it was as if she were answering his mental argument: "Oh, sure, a few people can get away with covering up the problem, but it's pretty costly in emotional and mental energy. All of their lives, they have to be on the

36

alert. It's like being a fugitive. Afraid of being caught, found out, exposed."

Josh stiffened but held onto his thought. But it can be done! She'd said it herself; it can be done! He wanted to lash out the words: You tripped yourself up, lady. I knew you would. I knew if I kept quiet, you'd talk yourself into a corner. But he'd promised himself to be careful and he held his words back.

"The trouble is," Mary went on, "if left untreated, the disfluency usually gets worse." She paused. "It's generally progressive."

There was silence now, the two of them staring at each other. Josh dropped his eyes first. Her words clanged in his head: Progressive . . . generally progressive!

Now she was saying something else but he couldn't hear her. Why didn't she shut up? Stop it! Shut up! First she says there's a way around it; then she pulls the rug up from under. Progressive? She made it sound like some kind of filthy disease! Why didn't she stop talking? He wanted to put his hands to his ears, block out the sound of her voice.

"Josh?"

He wouldn't look at her.

"Josh, listen. I told you all the rotten stuff first. So you'd know exactly what you're up against." She paused for a brief moment, then went softly on. "The hardest thing is to admit, to confront the problem. But if you can do that, if you're willing to do that, you can lick it. I can help you, show you how."

She was standing in front of him but still he wouldn't look at her. "It won't be easy. It'll be hard work. It won't be quick. But you can do it. You can help yourself."

He didn't know how long he sat there. Something had happened to him, but he couldn't make out what it was. What had gone wrong? He'd done exactly what he had planned to do. He hadn't said a word. He had let her do all the talking.

Then why did he feel as if he'd been punched out, drained? Why did he feel as if he'd just lost a major battle? And most baffling of all, why was he experiencing a strange kind of relief?

He started when he felt her hand on his shoulder. "That's all for today," he heard her say.

Josh stood up. She thrust the orange-colored paperback into his hands. "Don't forget the book," she said.

Chapter Six

For days afterward, his last session with Mary Taubin haunted him. What a downer. What a total downer. And what if she were right and he were wrong? What if he really did have a speech problem? No, no way, he didn't have a speech problem! But what if it got worse like she said it might? What if he blocked off completely, couldn't speak at all without fumbling. Impossible. Oh, yeah, how much impossible? What if it *was* progressive like Mary Taubin said? No, that was too scary. Anyway, none of that junk applied to him!

Besides, everybody bumbled words when they got excited, friends of his, guys he knew, it happened all the time. All right, so which guys and when did it happen all the time?

Knock it off, Josh, you're getting really creepy!

He wasn't aware of what he'd been doodling in his notebook. Miss Fletcher, the history teacher, was going on about John Brown, the abolitionist, and how Brown made his last stand at Harper's Ferry.

Josh looked at the doodle. It was a picture of a scaffold with a limp John Brown being hanged by the neck. Wow, how far down can you get? Josh ripped the page out of the notebook, rolled it into a ball, and stuffed it in his pocket.

He looked out the window. It was raining.

Rain in California was different from rain in other places. Rain in California was an event, a front-page item. Cars skidded, canyon streams became raging rivers, hillsides slid, houses lost their foundations. Rain was very big in California.

But people who weren't disaster victims loved it. The

first rain was exciting, eventful. Kids out of school liked to run in it bareheaded, getting sopped to the skin.

Josh wandered away from John Brown and let his head take him out of the classroom and into the rain. He was a rain lover. Howie was too. First rain, they'd go down to the creek near the house and watch the gentle little stream turn into a raging torrent.

One year, the big disaster year, there was a real killer rain. Josh would never forget that one. Howie either. Josh was fourteen, Howie nine. It began raining just after Howie's birthday. It rained three days, four days, six days.

Every day the headlines got bigger. Somerville Canyon, about a mile from their house, was the hardest hit. The two-lane road that wound down the canyon was now the bottom of a raging river that was carrying mud, timber, parts of houses, and automobiles in a terrifying deluge. Newsreels showed cars tumbling on their sides down the road, houses slowly disappearing in mountains of mud.

"Let's go," Howie said as Josh turned off the TV.

"No way," Josh said. "You heard the guy, no one goes in the canyon, they've got it blocked."

"We could go the back way, over the hill."

"Uh-uh," Josh said.

"I'd wear my boots."

"Nothing doing."

"And we could take my compass that I got for my birthday and make out we're lost, and you could lead us back to safety."

Josh laughed. "No way, Howie."

So Josh went back to the bedroom to tackle his homework, and when he looked out the window a few minutes later, there was Howie, boots and all, going over the back fence and up the hill.

Josh caught up with him half way up the incline. The rain was pelting down, but Howie was standing there calmly, looking at the compass.

"There's north," Howie said, pointing.

Josh shook his head in resignation. The kid was crazy. "You coming home?" Josh asked patiently.

"No, I'm going to Somerville Canyon." He closed the

compass case, grinned up at Josh. "You'd better come along so I won't get hurt or anything."

They went over the hill and down the back way to Somerville Canyon. They could hear the roar of the newly made river that had been Somerville Road, and through the trees they could see flashing lights of police cars and ambulances.

They worked their way higher up, not wanting to come out near the police cars. Most of the residents of the canyon had been evacuated earlier. Some houses stood with open doors, as water swept into once elegant living rooms.

They came out of the trees and close to the edge of the roaring torrent of churning brown water. It was hard to believe the terrible speed, the violent, twisting, battering strength of it.

Down the road, now a roiling rapid, the police had swung a rescue line over the water and a last resident, an elderly woman, was being pulled across on a harness, deputies waiting with outstretched hands to pull her to safety.

"Holy cow," Howie said, "look at that."

Josh was already watching the rescue. "We'd better get out of here," he said.

"Yeah, I guess we better," Howie agreed.

What was happening was exciting, but it was also scary and unpredictable, for anything could happen.

As they turned away, something caught Howie's eye. He stopped and came back to the edge of the water. There was a log jam of trees about six feet from the edge of the rain-created river. A small white cat was clinging to a broken tree trunk in the jam. The cat was mewing but the sound was muted under the roar of the water.

"Look!" Howie called, pointing to the cat.

Josh came back, and before he could even yell a warning, Howie had plunged into the water, clinging to a swaying tree trunk.

"Howie! Come out of there!"

The tree trunk swung with the current, clung for a moment to the pile of debris, and then let go.

41

Josh jumped in and grabbed at the tree trunk. "Hold on!" he screamed.

Howie's arms went around the trunk. The water seized it, flung the tree into the middle of the torrent. The river was a live thing, angry, violent, twisting the trunk, hurling it against the rushing debris.

Josh worked his way down the trunk to Howie, grabbed hold of the belt on Howie's parka. The trunk slammed against the newly made embankment. Howie went under; Josh sank with him, still hanging onto the belt. Finding a foothold on a sunken rock, Josh pulled Howie up. When they surfaced, the trunk was gone.

Josh held onto the belt grimly. The wild, churning current tumbled them over and over. He heard Howie cry out. Something sharp scraped his own side, rough stones banged, pelted at his legs. Desperately, he hung onto Howie's belt.

Suddenly they were slapped hard against a spongy, wet surface. It was a sofa standing on its end, wedged between a boulder and the skeleton of a car.

Josh, sputtering, spitting, still clutching onto Howie's belt, grasped the edge of the sofa and pulled Howie's upper body out of the water.

Coughing, gasping for air, Howie threw both arms around Josh's neck, clinging against him.

Josh disengaged one of Howie's arms and looked around. If they could get up onto the sofa; if they could get into the crevice between the seat and the back, they'd be safe. Tugging on Howie's belt, Josh shouted above the roar of the water. "Up! Climb up!"

With Josh lifting him by the belt, Howie pulled himself from out of the water and onto the sofa. Then he reached over and dragged Josh up to the safety of the water-soaked, bulging sofa.

The boys then saw the wildly gesturing deputies on the bank. The police harness dropped a few feet beside them, dancing crazily on the water. As the harness swirled closer, Josh made a grab for it. The sofa pitched dangerously.

"Hurry!" Josh yelled as he started to put Howie into the harness.

Howie held the harness between them, shook his head. "No! Both of us!" he screamed back between spasms of coughing.

A pounding crash of water sent the sofa teetering and the two boys, both holding onto the harness, slid down into the water.

Slowly, they were pulled over and into the out-stretched arms of the deputies.

As they were being draped in dry blankets, they saw a bedraggled, drenched white cat slink swiftly away between two police cars.

On the way home in the squad car, Josh tried to frame a plausible story for his mother, but he knew they were in for it. As the car bounced over the rain-made ruts, Howie leaned against Josh, his long hair like a wet mop on Josh's shoulder.

Josh felt good about Howie; the kid was wild but he really had guts, risking his neck like that to save a stupid cat.

Howie lolled against Josh, and just before he fell asleep, he thought what a great guy Josh had been, risking his neck for a stupid kid.

Anything could happen when it rained in California. Josh heard the bell ring for the end of the class. He got up and looked out the window. It was still raining. He could run home in the rain. That would really be neat.

It sat there on the desk, seeming to crouch like a fat, white monster. The receiver was the ears and the dial was a round, leering mouth. His telephone.

He hadn't wanted an extension in the bedroom, but Sandra had given it to him when he was fourteen as a symbol of independence, of growing up. He hated the thing. As soon as he lifted the receiver his pulse would race and he'd mumble every other word.

But now he had this new problem. The Lisa Schiller problem. After class she had given him back his history notes and he had said, trying to be casual, "Wuh, what about a muh . . . muh . . . movie sometime?" And she hadn't seemed to notice that he stumbled on the words

43

and she said, just as casually, "Love to. Give me a call,
I'm in the book." As if he didn't know she was in the
book. He had looked up her number long ago. In fact,
he knew it by heart: Lisa Schiller, 555-2720.

If he could just pick up the thing and say, "Hi, Lisa,
this is Josh. There's a great Robert Redford flick at the
Avon on Friday. I thought maybe you and I could have
a look." He liked the "Robert Redford flick," it sounded
casual, as if he had called her on a passing impulse instead of standing at the phone three days running without the nerve to lift the receiver.

One thing he could do. He had been skirting around
the idea, examining it for possible slip-ups. What he
could do was write it out on a piece of paper. Rehearse
it, kind of. After he had said the "Robert Redford flick"
he'd let her take over and he could get away with
"yeah" and "sure" and "okay."

It would probably work. Yeah, it probably would. He
sat down at the desk and began writing it out in large
printed letters on yellow paper. He just got down the
first few words when the phone rang.

The crouching monster had jumped up, attacked him.
He sat there as the bell jangled insistently. He could
ignore it, let it expel its venom helplessly. There was
nobody home. Carmela had taken Howie to the dentist
to have his teeth cleaned. Let it ring. But he wasn't that
brave. Supposing something had happened to Howie,
and Carmela was calling.

He picked up the phone. "Huh . . . hello."

"Hello." He heard a familiar voice on the other end.
"Who is this?"

"Juh . . . Juh . . . Joshua."

"Hi, Josh, it's me, Bill. I'm calling from Skytop. Is
Howie there?"

Josh struggled to say, "N . . . n̄ . . . no."

"Josh . . . ?"

Josh took a deep breath. "N . . . no, Buh . . . Buh . . .
Bill. He's at the duh . . . duh . . . dentist."

"Okay," Bill said cheerily. "I'll talk to you. How have
you been, Josh?"

"Fuh . . . fine." Josh said.

44

"And Sandra . . . your mother?"

"Okay," Josh managed to say.

"Well, good, good. Listen, you tell her I miss her, huh, Josh?"

Josh nodded, saving his breath.

"Joshua?"

"Yeah?"

"Listen, tell Howie I've found us a beautiful condo up here in Skytop. It'll be ready any day now. Tell him he's going to love it up here, Josh. And we had snow yesterday. I'm going to get him a pair of full-length skis. And tell him there are lots of kids up here, year-round kids. He'll have plenty of friends."

Josh drew a deep breath; his stomach began to tie up in knots.

"Josh . . . you there?"

"Yeah."

"Josh, listen, I know Howie'll miss you at first but you can come up and visit any time you want. Okay, Josh?"

He wanted to yell, it's not okay; it stinks! Why did you do this to us, to Howie and me! Tears of anger, frustration and rage filled his eyes.

"Joshua," said Bill, "I really mean that. You can visit any time."

"O . . . okay," he mumbled.

"Josh, tell Howie I love him and I'll call some other time, and don't forget to tell him it snowed here yesterday. He'll get a kick out of that."

"I . . . I'll tuh . . . tuh . . . tell him."

"Bye, Josh. Take care. And give my love to your mother."

Josh nodded to the phone. It clicked off. He put down the receiver, wiped his eyes with the back of his hand. He trembled with rage at the selfish, me-me, life-of-my-own, uncaring grownups. Grownups? What was really grown up about them? All they wanted was fun, just like kids. And they wanted big things: cars, houses, clothes, trips. And they wanted each other till they got tired of each other, and then they wanted someone new. Why haven't grownups ever really grown up?

The front door slammed. He could hear Howie racing

back to the bedroom. He ducked into the bathroom to douse his face with water.

"Hey, Josh . . ."

Howie poked his head past the bathroom door. He showed his teeth in a fierce grin. "Look, Josh, no cavities!"

Josh came out wiping his face with a towel.

Howie pulled a dollar out of his pants pocket, waved it at Josh. "Carmela gave it to me for not yelling about the dentist."

He went to the desk, stuffed the dollar into a small drawer. "We can get her a new rosary for Christmas, okay?"

"Okay," Josh said.

Howie sat at the desk, pulled out his geography book and opened to the assignment.

"Howie . . ."

"Yeah?"

Josh hesitated a moment. "Bill called to talk to you just a while ago."

Howie turned from his geography book, a worried look on his face.

"He said to tell you it snowed there yesterday."

Howie's worried look didn't change. "It snowed."

"Yeah, and . . ."

"When do I have to go?" Howie asked.

Josh took a deep breath. "Howie, listen to me. This isn't going to be so bad. It really isn't. I mean you'll find lots of friends up there, and you can ski . . ."

"When do I have to go?" Howie said.

"Look, it's not tomorrow . . ."

"Maybe you want it to be tomorrow."

"I didn't say . . ."

Howie got up from the desk. "Maybe it's okay with you if I go up there right now so I can ski and have new friends. And . . . and . . . and who needs you, anyway!"

Howie stalked out of the room.

Josh sat down on the bed. Rotten! All the selfish, me-me, uncaring grownups. Rotten! All of them!

Chapter Seven

Josh began to worry about the book Mary Taubin had given him, the orange-colored paperback. Like that bad penny people laughed about, it kept turning up everywhere.

When he first brought it home, Josh flung it into his closet and watched it land on the floor next to his boots in the corner. But then, every time he opened the closet door, the book all but leaped up at him. The bright, orange rectangle seemed almost phosphorescent, like a traffic beacon in the dark.

The next morning Josh had kicked the book behind the laundry hamper. Then it showed up on the middle of his desk after Carmela found it on vacuuming day. He elbowed it aside to make room for his algebra homework. But the bright orange cover glowed malevolently at him, distracting him from x multiplied by $2y$. Its very title was demanding, offensive: *SPEAK UP*, it screamed in bold, black letters. *SPEAK UP*.

Finally Josh took up the book, turned it over in his hands. What had Taubin said? Oh, yeah, "You'll find lots of information about speech disorders in there."

Speech disorders. He had all the information he needed to know, more than he wanted to know. He pushed the book aside and bent over his algebra. But his head wouldn't let him concentrate on x multiplied by $2y$. For some reason his eyes kept drifting over to the hated orange paperback. *SPEAK UP*, it admonished.

"Speak up," the ticket seller said impatiently. Ten-year-old Josh had been left at the movies that Saturday afternoon, and he finally made his way to the front of the line.

"Speak up! Movie 1, 2, or 3?" the lady in the booth snapped.

They were showing an old rerun of *Tarzan and the Apes* in movie 2. That was the one Josh wanted to see. He tried for the word: "Tuh ... tuh ... tuh ... tuh ..."

"Come on, let's go!" said a big boy in line behind him.

Josh panicked, swallowed, tried again. "Nuh ... nuh ... nuh ... number two!" he blasted louder than he had intended.

As he bolted for the entrance, Josh could hear the boy behind him laughing.

He dove into the darkness of the theater, stumbled into a vacant seat in the last row. He began to relax, breathe a little easier as the coming attractions were screened.

Then the kids in front of him hollered and clapped at the beginning of the cartoon. Josh laughed with the rest of the children at the sight of an ugly red bird on the screen. But then the bird spoke: "D ... d ... d ... dah ... dah ... d ... d ... d ... dah, ... dah ..."

The audience screamed and howled delightedly. "D ... d ... d ... dah ... dah ..." the woodpecker stuttered raucously.

Roaring laughter followed Josh as he plunged into the aisle and made his way to the men's room.

And there he stayed for a long while only going back when he was sure the feature had started.

Josh sighed heavily. Yeah, he knew all he wanted to know about speech disorders. He knew firsthand. Yet, without his willing it, he picked up the oranged-colored paperback, opened the book, and began to read.

Mary Taubin was sitting at her desk. "Ready?" she asked.

Josh looked at her belligerently. He was as ready as he'd ever be. He'd come to these idiotic sessions, listened to her drone on and on about speech disfluencies, blockages. He'd read the orange-colored paperback book from beginning to end. He was ready, all right. Now, let's see how ready she was. Go ahead, he thought. Do your magic. Cure me. You're the expert. Prove it.

"Josh?"

"Ruh . . . ruh . . . ready," he said forcibly, irritably.

"Good." She gave him a book. "Read."

Josh let her tape his voice while he read. He answered her questions: When had he first started to stutter? How did he feel about it? What methods did he use to try to combat it? Hide it? What was his mother's attitude about it? Were there some sounds or words that continually gave him trouble? Did his stuttering usually occur on the first sound or syllable? What usually precipitated trouble? Was he afraid of speaking? Embarrassed?

There were more questions. And still more. Some of them made sense to Josh; some seemed off the wall, crazy, unnecessary. But he answered them all. Then came the one question he was really ready for. He'd rehearsed it in his mind, knowing it would come sooner or later.

"When is your mother coming in to see me, Josh?"

"Cuh . . . can't . . . her b . . . b . . . busy season. Sh . . . she'll help me at home."

"That's all right. I'll telephone her at . . ."

"No! Duh . . . duh . . . duh . . . don't do that!"

Mary looked at him closely.

"She's tuh . . . tuh . . . tuh . . . too busy," Josh ended lamely.

Mary nodded.

Then Josh sat back and waited for the next question. But she just looked at him silently, expectantly.

And suddenly, without any more prompting, without any more prodding, he really let loose. Striding back and forth before her desk, he sputtered out the old hurts, the memories of being teased, laughed at, put down, the butt of lousy jokes. The special memory. Being left at school for the first time, how he had cried, sobbed, been terrified his mother would never come back. How the other kids had called him baby. How he had tripped over his words in anger, in his fear, in his shame. And the kids had laughed, called him Porky Pig. The teacher had stopped the teasing and the children

49

soon forgot about it. But Josh didn't forget. He had never forgotten.

Now, stammering, tripping over words, whole phrases, he told her about the telephone phobia, about the inexplicable times when his speech was perfect, when he could talk without stumbling, when he could read aloud to Howie, perfectly, normally. He told her about the times he had trouble, when he was uptight, on the spot, anxious. He told her how he clammed up when he felt frustrated, defeated. He told her how it was getting harder and harder to speak without stuttering ever since the talk about divorce at home, ever since he knew Howie would be leaving. And it was getting worse, worse all the time.

What made her think she could help him? Nobody could! It was too late, impossible! Kids in his class noticed. Miss Deemers noticed. Everyone noticed!

Taubin listened, let him spill, let him rage until he wound down, sank back into his chair. He sat hunched over, depleted, drained, feeling hollow. Then: "I'm a fuh ... fuh ... fuh ... freak," he said dully.

"Look at me, Josh."

He looked at her, expecting to see a smug smile on her face, contempt, disgust, or worse, pity.

But what he saw in her eyes was something else. It wasn't disgust. It wasn't pity.

It was understanding, caring. She cared.

In the sessions that followed, they went to work. At first Josh hated the emotion-charged periods. He hated them; at times he hated her.

He detested what she did, how she stuttered for him, showing him how to stammer easily. Josh balked. He already knew how to stutter! What he didn't know was how *not* to stutter!

But she insisted that he ape her, made him repeat after her while she exploded a word out, made him mimic her as she struggled, elongated her vowels, fumbled, blocked. Then she made him say the same word, bouncing it deliberately, but softer, easier.

50

Some days he fought her, yelled at her. She fought back, yelled back. But she persisted. She cared.

Session after session, she fell in and out of various speech patterns herself; she machine-gunned her sentences, literally popping out the words, forcing them, blasting them. She demonstrated all the ways there were to foul a word up, all the ways Josh fouled up *his* words. And then she said the same words smoothly, softly, sliding the sentences out in loose, stammering, syrupy strings. And she never let up until he repeated the sentences after her, matching her stammering sound for sound.

Over and over, she made him listen to his early reading tapes. Over and over she made him retape the same reading passages, made him listen for any differences, any changes.

His patience tried, Josh was angered and bored by turns. Sometimes she met his anger with a fury of her own. Sometimes she met his sullen muteness with an implacable, immutable silence.

At times Taubin held a mirror up to Josh's mouth while he watched his own lips clamp down on a word, his own tongue jam against his teeth. She pointed out the spasms he created, made him aware of the block, made him feel the air-flow, stay with it until he gained control, make the words come out the way he willed them.

He railed at her, smart-mouthed her, wasted her time and his time. He came to sessions late; he quit early. She told him he was behaving like a baby pulling temper tantrums. She told him he could quit therapy altogether, but that she cared. Even when he behaved as if *he* didn't care, she told him, she did. She cared.

She demonstrated how to take a moment of hard stuttering and, like an acrobat, do a pull-out, turn it into an easier form. She forced him to face his stuttering head-on, to make a conscious effort to manipulate it, gain control over it, direct it to his will.

And there were the seemingly endless exercises of prolonging words, vowels, stretching them, bending them over and over. Over and over until Josh could hardly stand the sound of her voice. Until he'd had it one day and ran from the room vowing never to come back.

But still he came back. He knew she cared and he came back. Now, he began to think of the sessions as a kind of endurance test, a trial of wills. Would he break first? Or would Mary Taubin?

And then they began what Josh came to think of as the "field tests." Mary took him off campus to the malt shop, ordered a Coke for both of them. And while they were enjoying the Cokes, she nonchalantly told him that next time, *he'd* be doing the talking, he'd do the ordering. This angered him. What was she trying to pull? She knew only too well how hard it was for him to talk in public places. But the next time, Josh did do it. He ordered double banana splits for both of them, the most expensive item on the menu. But she paid the tab happily, applauding his courage for doing it despite his embarrassment, despite his stammering.

Another day, she led him into the post office and stood by with obvious pride as he painfully asked for information regarding special delivery service.

And there was the day they went to the school library, Josh requesting various tricky-sounding titles while she signalled her approval in suppressed giggles.

There was the time they walked to the corner, and Josh stopped a total stranger to ask directions to town. Gleefully, Mary supported his charade by repeating the directions and heartily thanking the passerby.

Josh was always reluctant to perform on these crazy, weird field trips, yet he found that the encounters were gradually becoming easier, more comfortable, less and less threatening. Sometimes he performed perfectly, fluently. Sometimes he stuttered badly. But always Mary was delighted. The world didn't turn on whether he stuttered or not, she joyously pointed out. The world didn't care. And Josh knew she was right. And it didn't matter to him whether the world cared or not. He knew that she cared. Mary Taubin cared.

The sessions slowly became more tolerable for Josh. Once in a while he even looked forward to the speech period. He was making progress. He began to see a noticeable difference in his everyday exchanges with kids at school, the family at home. He rejoiced in the discovery that a whole day could go by once in a while without a single stuttered word. And on days like this he almost dared to hope . . . to believe that some day he'd be able to speak fluently, normally. The sessions took a bright, new turn. Until the day of the telephone.

The day of the telephone wiped out all his newly acquired, fragile confidence. The day Mary Taubin watched while Josh took her place at her desk and hesitantly reached out to pick up the phone. He was to call and get detailed information on how to apply for an advertised job.

Holding the phone in a sweaty grip, he dialed the number. Why had he agreed to make the call? He'd never be able to talk into the thing. He'd always had trouble with the phone. Always. And now, with Mary watching, expecting him to do well, it was doubly hard.

He heard the ringing on the other end. Maybe no one would answer. Maybe they were closed for the day. Then someone said, "Personnel, may I help you?"

"Th . . . th . . . th . . . I . . . I . . . I . . . I . . ." He couldn't. He couldn't do it.

"Hello? May I help you?"

"Your name," Mary whispered. "Say your name."

"Juh . . . juh . . . juh . . ." He was helpless, totally blanked out. All he had learned, everything he had been taught, flew out of his head. He flicked a panicked look at Mary. She smiled encouragingly. Into the phone, he said, "Thu . . . thu . . . the job. I . . . I . . . I . . . I . . . I . . ." His throat constricted, his teeth clamped down hard, his jaw went rigid.

"Hello . . . hello . . ." the voice on the phone repeated.

Josh loosened his grip on the phone. It slipped out of his hand, dangled over the desk. He stared at it as it spun crazily. Mary picked it up and put it back on its cradle.

Slowly Josh wiped his damp hands on his jeans. He felt a dull throbbing at his temples, a sickening feeling in his stomach.

Then he felt Mary's hand on his shoulder. "It's all right, Josh. It's okay."

He couldn't look at her. He had failed. It was all for nothing. All the therapy. All the work. A bust. He kept his eyes fixed on the phone.

"Josh, it's only the beginning of a long road," Mary said. "You didn't make it this time. It doesn't matter. Who cares?"

Chapter Eight

It came suddenly, like a telegram announcing death. Bill had called Sandra. The condo in Skytop was ready, he had registered Howie at Skytop Junior High School and he'd be there to pick Howie up at noon the next day.

Sandra got the call at her office. For a moment she considered telling Bill it was too quick, too hurtful for the boys, only one day's notice. But the moment passed. After all, Howie was Bill's kid and if he was going to take him, better get it over with fast. A quick surgical cut. It would bleed a lot but probably heal faster.

When she put down the phone she thought for another moment of going home, being there when Josh got back from school, telling him herself. But Carmela was so much better at those things. Carmela could deal with it.

So she picked up the phone again, dialed her home, and told Carmela. Then she said Carmela could start getting Howie's things together.

Howie's duffle bag stood up in the middle of the bedroom, its gaping mouth hungrily gulping clothes, boots, sweaters, valuable junk long hidden in the backs of closets.

Howie pulled the cord on his electric clock. Time stood still at ten-thirty. He dumped the clock into the bag.

Josh held out a camera, a Polaroid with flash.

"Why don't you take this?" he said.

"Uh-uh, that's yours."

"You take it, send me pictures."

"Uh-uh, that was your birthday present."

Josh put the camera in the duffle bag.

"I don't know how to work it," Howie said.

"Bill will show you. Just send pictures, that's all."

"Okay. Thanks, Josh."

"Stuff it," Josh said smiling.

"Stuff it yourself," Howie said, returning the smile.

Josh put a pack of film in with the camera. "Maybe it's a good thing you're going to a new school, you're learning too much dirty talk."

"I learned it from you," Howie said.

Josh gave Howie a soft brotherly kick in the behind and Howie returned it with a backhand slap at Josh's gut as Sandra opened the door.

"Ten-thirty, Josh. Howie's got a long day tomorrow."

"O . . . okay, Mom."

She stepped into the room, looked at the disarray. "Have you got everything, Howie?"

"I guess so."

Sandra glanced in the top of the duffle bag.

"I guh . . . guh . . . gave him my camera. O . . . okay, Mom?"

"Of course, Joshua."

She looked around the room, then bent down and put her arms around Howie. "I'm going to miss you, Howie," she said. And for that moment she really meant it.

Howie looked up at her. She kissed the top of his forehead. "Goodnight, Howie."

" 'Night," Howie said.

She kissed the top of Josh's head, closed the door softly.

Howie pulled the drawstrings around the duffle bag.

"I left my skateboard in the garage," Howie said. "You use it."

"No, you take it."

"What am I going to do, skate in the snow?"

"Okay," Josh said, "I'll use it."

"Don't break your butt."

"I'll try not to."

Howie leaned the duffle bag against the bunk. He took off his shoes and trousers, then crawled in.

"You want to read to me, Josh?"

"Okay," Josh said. He took the space book off the desk.

"Unless you've got homework," Howie said.

"Tomorrow's Saturday."

"Oh, yeah. Saturday. Monday I'll be in a new school."

"Yeah, Monday."

Howie put his head back on the pillow. "Okay," he said.

"Where were we?" Josh asked.

"The spaceship Airon was approaching the gravitational field of Septarus."

Josh thumbed the pages, found the place. He smiled at Howie who had closed his eyes, shutting out earthly things.

" 'They lowered the third force rockets into the firing bay. No one could tell what lay behind the glowing rings around Septarus. In moments they would enter the gravitational field and make their orbit around the unknown planet.' "

Josh read on, not hearing the words he was saying, feeling numb, empty, defeated. In less than five minutes, when the spaceship Airon was seeing weird flashes of greenish fire coming from Septarus, Howie was asleep.

Josh closed the book. He leaned over, opened the drawstrings of the duffle bag, worked the book down under the sweaters, then closed the drawstrings.

For several minutes he looked at Howie, then turned off the light and climbed up into his bunk, not taking off his clothes. He lay there looking up into black nothingness. He heard the hall clock strike eleven, twelve, one. He must have fallen asleep briefly. He heard four. Then, when he had counted five he got down from the bunk and groped in the predawn dark for his running shoes.

It was still dark when he began the long agonizing run.

There was no plan to the run, no awareness of where he was going. Speed was all. Angry, punishing speed into the darkness. At the bottom of the hill he ran into the boulevard, not seeing, not caring about the headlights of the car that could easily have closed out his life.

More speed. Out onto the beach highway, pounding the shoulder of the road. Early morning workers caught him in their lights, heads shook. Those runners, nuts, the whole bunch of them.

Down the highway faster, his breath coming in gulps. No pacing now, no running to win. Just speed, more speed.

Habit brought him across the highway and onto the beach. The sand fought his legs. He fought back, driving his shoes in deep with every step. He gasped for breath, choosing the loose sand for his adversary, rejecting the easy, hard-packed stuff near the water.

A sharp pain hit him in the groin. He gasped, kept on, stumbling now and then on the small hillocks of sand. Then the burning sensation in his thighs. The sand seemed to get heavier, to have unseen hands trying to pull him down. He felt sick as he gulped the air.

On and on, mile after mile, down the empty beach, under the pier, along the hard cement walkway, past the shuttered refreshment stands, unaware of the sun coming up, the blinds raised by early-morning people in the beachfront apartments.

Back on the sand. And then the beer can lying flat. Waiting there. His foot hit the can. He went down with his face in the sand and that's all he remembered.

He lay there for hours, face down. The skaters along the concrete path saw him, a kid sunning himself. The cyclists passed him by. Lucky kid, lying face down in the sun.

The beach patrol car moved slowly past on its morning round. The passenger cop tapped his driver. The car stopped; the cop got out. Something about the way the kid was lying there. An O. D. maybe?

He touched Josh on the shoulder. "You all right, son?"

He rolled him over. The kid was out, just barely breathing.

The patrol car backed up. The driver called the paramedics. The other cop looked down at Josh, shook his head slowly. "What they do to themselves. You just can't believe it, can you?"

The best the doctor could come up with was "nervous exhaustion." So Josh lay there, in Howie's bunk, the lower bunk because it was more convenient when Carmela tried to feed him eggnogs and stuff him with vitamins.

He didn't read or listen to the stereo, or look at TV. He just lay there with the blinds drawn and slept a lot. He didn't know how many days it was. He just remembered worried faces looking down at him, asking how he felt and not knowing how he felt, just lying there surrounded by nothingness.

The day of the final cross-country trials came and went. Josh was only mildly surprised that he didn't care about missing the trials, that it didn't hurt, even when he learned later that Eddie Lenz came in first and was elected captain pro tem till spring. Nothing much mattered anymore.

But one evening, maybe a week later, maybe longer, Sandra came into the room. She was smiling encouragingly about something. She picked up the phone, held it out to him.

"Someone for you," she said.

He drew back from the phone, his enemy, but Sandra went on, "It's Howie, calling from Skytop."

He propped himself up on one elbow as Sandra put the phone on his bunk and left the room.

Josh looked at the phone, waited for the dreaded tightening in his throat. But this was Howie calling. He could talk to Howie.

"Hello," Josh said.

"Hi, Josh, it's me, Howie, how are you, listen, this is a dumb school, the kids are dumb, I got in a fight with a kid named Herman, Bill said you're sick, are you sick, Josh? What are you sick with? I had a cold and a runny nose and this jerk, Herman, called me snot-nose so I plugged him."

"I suppose he was bigger than you," Josh said.

"Yeah, I guess so. How's Carmela?"

"She's fine."

"Josh, listen, I hate this school, but Bill wouldn't like it if I took off."

"Howie . . ."

"Yeah?"

"Never mind the taking-off stuff, you stay in school."

"Why?"

"Howie . . ."

"Okay, okay, I'll stay. Listen, Josh . . ."

"Yeah."

"Did they tell you? About Christmas?"

"No."

"They've got it worked out. I'm coming down."

Josh felt a sudden lift of elation. "Christmas?"

"Yeah. I think you're going someplace for a week, then I'm coming there for Christmas."

"I'm going someplace?"

"Something like that. Then we have Christmas. Listen, I know what we'll get Carmela. A guy here makes a neat manger set with lights and a flock of angels and animals. Nine dollars."

Josh sat up straighter. "Okay, I'll go half."

"I already bought it. You can pay me Christmas. Bill just came in. He wants to say hello."

Bill came on, asked Josh how he was, sent his love to Sandra, his best to Carmela, and handed the phone back to Howie.

"Josh . . . I gotta go. We're going to the movies."

Josh smiled, still warmed by the thought of Christmas. "Okay, Howie, have fun. And listen . . ."

"I know, I know," Howie said, and Josh could feel the warm smile in his brother's voice. "I'll stay in the dumb school, don't worry."

"Okay. So long, Howie."

"See you Christmas," Howie said.

The phone clicked off. Josh put down the receiver. He swung his legs carefully over the bunk and stood up. He felt wobbly, but he walked across the room slowly and stood looking out the window at the clear, starry night.

Maybe he'd take a walk tomorrow. Maybe even jog a

few steps. Yeah, maybe he'd do that. Not too much, say ten steps walking, ten steps jogging. Go into it easy.

He turned from the window, put on his bathrobe. All of a sudden he was hungry. Maybe he'd go down and see what Carmela had to eat.

He made it back to school but he was still a little foggy. After his last class he turned in the direction of Howie's old school and was halfway down the block before he remembered. But things got a little better each day and at the end of the week he was making all his classes, including speech therapy, and even jogging a little on the school track.

He liked the jogging. It was undemanding and the steady run was restful. You didn't have to think too much when jogging, just go with your feet.

One afternoon he was alone on the track except for this girl somewhere behind him. Or it looked like a girl. Well, you couldn't really tell, somebody's body was all wrapped up in a gray sweatsuit, and all you could see was a fuzzy mop of red hair. He was curious, so he slowed up a little.

"Hi," said the red-haired runner.

It was Mary Taubin!

"Wuh . . . wuh . . . what the . . . huh . . . huh . . ."

Mary laughed. "What the *heck* am I doing here? I'm jogging just like you."

Josh smiled. "I . . . I duh . . . didn't know . . ."

"I usually go late in the day." She fell into step with him. "How you feeling, Josh?"

"O . . . okay."

"Good." She set her watch. "I've got to do this one in eight minutes. Come along?"

He grinned. "Sure." An eight-minute mile was barely moving for Josh.

They swung into it. Mary had a nice easy stride and she picked up her heels smartly. Josh liked the way she ran, very contained, economical, no puff or strain.

The eight minutes went swiftly. It was friendly, running with someone. Like dancing, sharing the same rhythm and movement.

At the end of the mile they jogged over to the benches and sat down. Josh looked at her admiringly. "You . . . you run real nice."

"Thanks." She wiped the sweat off her face with her sleeve, looked at her watch. "I'm going to cut five seconds every day till I get down to seven and a half."

"Easy," he said.

"For you," she answered.

"You too. Juh . . . juh . . . just a little every day. Luh . . . luh . . . like . . ."

"Like therapy," she said.

"Yeah," he said and they laughed comfortably.

Mary stood up. "I've got to go." She smiled down at him. "Are you here every day at this time?"

"I . . . could be."

"I might join you, okay?"

"Okay, Miss . . . Tau . . . Tau . . ." He stopped, held up his hand for her to wait. He breathed deeply for the effort, then said it perfectly.

"Okay, Mary."

Thanksgiving was a bummer without Howie. Josh tried to avoid the big home dinner. He asked his mother why didn't he and she eat at Chasen's or one of those other fancy places she went to. But she had already bought the turkey and had invited that creep, Jack Bender, to "share a family gathering."

Luckily the creep had to be in New York on business so Josh and his mother and Carmela had the turkey all to themselves.

They all wanted to make it festive, with Sandra particularly trying, but she acted as though she still felt the emptiness, remembering other years with Bill and Howie.

She opened a bottle of wine to help chase the gloom, even gave Josh a half-glass, which he didn't enjoy but drank to please her. Nervously, she kept pouring wine for herself and looking at the phone in the living room, as though hoping Jack might call.

A real bummer, that dinner.

But Sandra wouldn't give up; she wanted it to be festive, a holiday. Somewhere there ought to be one cheerful note.

Josh was aching to get away from the table when she said, out of the blue, "About Christmas vacation, Joshua . . ."

He sat up.

"Christmas vacation," she repeated, and smiled and drank the last of the wine. The whole bottle was gone. She set down her glass carefully. "Christmas," she said.

Josh was suddenly worried. "Huh . . . Howie will be here."

"Yes, of course," Sandra said.

He was relieved. He managed to smile at her.

She returned the smile. "But before Christmas . . ." She was slurring her words a little. ". . . week before Christmas . . . I thought maybe we'd go someplace. Like skiing."

"Skiing?"

"How about Winter Valley?"

"No . . . kuh . . . kidding?"

"Would you like that?"

Would he! Winter Valley was the ultimate in skiing. He had seen pictures of it. An Alpine village perched high in the Rockies, a new really spectacular resort, almost rivaling Aspen and a bit ridiculously but glowingly advertised as Switzerland West.

"Yeah," he said with a deep breath of pleasure. "Yeah, I'd like that."

She touched his hand fondly. "It'll put you back in shape again."

He laughed. "Ruh . . . roses in my cheeks."

She laughed too. When he was younger she used to run with him on the beach and tell him it put roses in his cheeks.

Then the phone rang in the living room. She jumped up. It had to be Jack Bender.

It was.

Josh couldn't help but hear the pleasure in her voice as she answered. The mental picture of Winter Valley snapped off as he was forced to listen to the intimate, secret laughter coming from the living room.

Josh pushed pieces of mince pie around on his plate. He wanted to get out of the dining room but he knew it would look funny if she came back from the call and he wasn't there.

Jack was doing most of the talking, but then he heard his mother say, "Yes, I told him, he's crazy to go, he adores skiing." There was a pause, then she said, "No, no, it's perfectly all right." Then a pause and she said something in a low voice and laughed and hung up.

She came back to the dining room, smiling. "That was Jack," she said.

Josh nodded.

She laughed lightly. "He'll be back Monday."

Josh couldn't look at her. "Is . . . is . . . huh . . . he . . ." He couldn't get the words out.

She waited patiently, pouring herself some more coffee.

"Is he . . . is . . . Juh . . . Jack guh . . . guh . . . going to Winter Valley?"

"Well, of course, darling. That's understood. You don't mind, do you?"

Josh took a deep breath.

"Yuh . . . yes."

"Yes, what?"

"Yuh . . . yes, I do mind. I . . . I thought . . ." He pulled in a large gulp of air.

"Say what you want to say, Joshua. Don't gulp."

It exploded out in one sentence. "I thought it was just you and me!"

She looked down into her coffee cup a long time. Then she said slowly. "What don't you like about Jack Bender, Joshua?"

Josh shook his head, unable to speak.

"I like Jack," Sandra said. "He's good company. He . . . he's spontaneous, fun. We have lots in common."

Then Josh started to get up from the table.

"Sit down, Joshua."

He sat, avoiding looking at her. He pushed his mince pie around the plate.

"Joshua, look at me."

He forced himself to look at her.

"We're going to Winter Valley, you and Jack and I. And we're going to have a marvelous time together. Jack is a terrific skier and he knows everybody and we've got reservations at the lodge. Joshua! Look at me!"

He got up from the table. "I . . . I don't want to go," he said slowly, deliberately.

He stood there looking down at her. Then, unbelievably, tears started rolling down her cheeks. She didn't move, didn't wipe the tears, just sat there crying helplessly.

He couldn't stand it. "I . . . I'm sorry."

"Joshua," she said softly, "I've worked so hard, I've worked so very hard."

"Mom . . ."

She gestured weakly around the room, knocking over the empty wine bottle, not noticing. "Ever since your father left, when you were hardly old enough to talk, ever since, I've worked . . ." She gestured again. ". . . and given you, us, all of this. I've been . . ." She tried to choose the word carefully. "I've been responsible, Joshua . . ."

He was embarrassed. He had never seen her cry before. He wanted to comfort her, put his arms around her, but he couldn't. A sense of guilt washed over him. If it weren't for him. . . .

"Responsible, Joshua."

She looked into her empty wine glass, twirled it between her fingers, talking as if Josh weren't there. As if she were remembering, thinking out loud. "I thought with Bill life could be . . . adventurous, joyful . . . and for a while . . ."

She paused, frowned. "My mother, father . . . it was horrible. Hating each other, sticking with it just for the kids, sticking to the bitter end . . ."

She shook her head, seemed to snap back from wherever she'd been.

"Responsible, Joshua. And now . . . now before it's too late . . ."

Carmela came in with a tray to take the dishes. Sandra got up quickly and left the room.

Carmela began putting the plates on the tray.

"Carmela . . ."

"Sí?"

"Whu . . . whu . . . where are my ski boots?"

"No requerdo? You do not remember? You give to Howie."

"Oh, yeah, I did."

"You must have ski boots?"

"Yeah. Mom and I are going skiing in Winter Valley." Carmela smiled. "Bueno, you will enjoy."

"Yeah . . . we're guh, guh, going to have a tuh . . . tuh . . . terrific time."

He got up from the table and started to gather dishes to help Carmela.

"I . . . I guess you can rent buh . . . boots in Winter Valley."

Chapter Nine

He kept thinking of Howie. It was the weekend before Christmas vacation and he decided to use the time to buy Howie a present. He knew just what Howie wanted. It was a rocket kit that practically guaranteed you could hit the moon on the first try. They had seen the ad many times in their science fiction magazine, and now the rocket was being offered at the big department store in Westwood.

Josh checked the two crisp twenty-dollar bills in the pocket of his jeans. They felt reassuring as he made his way to the toy department. The twenties were part of his Christmas Club money, half of it. The other half would go for his share of Carmela's present and something for his mother and Bill.

A huge Christmas tree stood at the entrance to the toy department; carols played relentlessly. The tree went unnoticed by most shoppers, going grimly on their way, getting it over early, doing their duty, paying heavy tribute to the unending tradition.

But Josh felt pretty good about it. He smiled at the tree, even imagined he could smell the wonderful scent of real pine needles. He forgot, for the moment, the problems, the sure-to-be-disastrous trip to Winter Valley. He let himself be caught up in the sounds and color and excitement of the holiday.

There it was on the top of a display case, the rocket model assembled in front of a display of boxes picturing a leap into space. He stood there, admiring the rocket, when he heard a small giggle behind him and felt a tap on his shoulder. He turned quickly.

It was Lisa Schiller standing there only inches away from him with this big smile on her face!

"Joshua Taylor, what are you doing here!"

That beautiful, dumb, idiotic question. It was wonderful. And in that instant before he answered, all the weeks with Mary Taubin flashed across the screen of his mind, all the hard work, the pain, the struggle. It all paid off. He answered, carefully, of course, but unflubbed. With brilliant clarity he said, "What are you doing here?"

And they both laughed.

"I'm getting something for my dumb kid sister," said Lisa. "She's only nine."

Josh felt as if he had been admitted to the innermost circle of her family. A dumb kid sister, of course. "Whu . . . what are you getting her?" he asked carefully.

"What do you suggest?" asked Lisa.

He couldn't believe it. Such immediate intimacy. She was asking him, Josh, for suggestions. Man, this is moving fast.

His eye lit on a display of dolls that wept on demand. "Why duh . . . don't you get her one of those?"

"Terrific," said Lisa. "She cries as much as the doll. Thanks ever, Josh, you're a real help."

Josh smiled, not risking a don't-mention-it.

Lisa made a move to go, then stopped. "Oh, Josh, I'm having a pre-Christmas party at my place. Could you make it?"

He wanted to jump for joy. Could he make it! He was going to say he sure could when he realized he'd be in Winter Valley.

He shook his head sadly. "I . . . I won't be here," he said.

"Oh," Lisa said. She sounded disappointed.

"I . . . I'm going to . . . to be in Winter Valley."

Lisa's eyes widened. She was impressed. "Winter Valley!"

"Yeah," Josh said. "Skiing."

"That's terrific," Lisa said.

And now he could see how impressed she was so he

risked a little more. "I . . . I'm getting a pair of Nordicas for Christmas."

Luckily, Lisa knew that Nordicas were ski boots.

"Terrific," said Lisa. "Well, look, maybe we'll work something out after you come back."

"Shu . . . sure thing," Josh said.

Lisa smiled and went off to the crying dolls.

He turned back to the display counter, his heart pumping as if he had just crossed the finish line of a ten-kilometer run. He had hardly flubbed a word. He glanced at Lisa over at the doll counter. Lisa Schiller, in person, and he had carried it off. Wow!

The college girl saleslady had been observing the exchange between Josh and Lisa. "May I help you?" she asked, with a friendly smile.

"Yeah," Josh said. He pointed to a packaged rocket. "I'll take one of those. Guh . . . gift-wrapped, please."

As the girl deftly wrapped the rocket box Josh watched Lisa. Evidently she decided against the doll. Maybe it wasn't worth all that money for a dumb kid sister. She turned toward the young people's clothes. He watched her move out of sight.

The saleslady put the package on the counter. Josh gave her the two twenties. The rocket was twenty-two seventy-five with tax. He took the change.

"Would you like an enclosure card?" asked the saleslady.

"Nuh . . . no, thanks," Josh said. "I . . . I'm going to make my own."

"Oh, that's nice," the saleslady said.

Josh smiled at her, patted the gaily wrapped package. "This is special. It . . . it's for my brother."

He left the toy department, seeming to walk a few feet above the floor. He thought maybe he'd look around the store, see if there was something he could find for his mother.

He wasn't really concentrating on it, just kind of floating around the store, holding onto his package, not even noticing several women who couldn't help smiling at this handsome boy who seemed to be so into Christmas.

And then, about a half hour later, it all fell apart. He was standing at the perfume counter wondering whether he should blow the rest of the money on some fancy bath soap for his mother, the kind she liked, when he saw Lisa Schiller coming toward him again. Eddie Lenz was holding her arm and even twenty yards away you could almost feel the intimacy. They stopped for a moment to look into a display case and Eddie put his arm around Lisa's waist as they bent over the case and their heads touched and they laughed.

As they straightened up from the case and came toward him he wanted to run but he couldn't.

"Hi," Eddie Lenz said, almost friendly.

Josh gulped, unable to answer.

"Don't forget to call me," Lisa said as they passed.

Josh nodded.

"Hey, Josh," Eddie said stopping a moment, still holding onto Lisa. "Where have you been, trackwise? Not coming out any more?"

"I . . . wah . . . was sick," Josh mumbled.

"Oh," said Eddie. "Tough. Well, Merry Christmas and all that."

"Muh . . . muh . . . muh . . . merry . . . Kuh . . . kuh . . . kuh . . ." He couldn't finish.

He watched them go out the front door. He couldn't hear their muffled laughter but he could see it; he could feel it through the glass door. *Muh . . . muh . . . merry Christmas.*

There wasn't any planning to it. No conscious decision. It happened when he opened his locker at noon and the orange paperback book fell at his feet. Without thinking, he picked it up and headed down the corridor.

He strode into the room without knocking. Mary Taubin was hunched over her desk, listening intently to her tape recorder.

Josh was aware of a girl's voice on the recorder as he approached Mary's desk. " . . . tuh . . . tuh . . . tuh . . . talking is . . . tuh . . . tuh . . . tuh . . . tuh . . ." the tape recorder said. There was a pause and it went on. ". . . tuh . . . tuh . . . tuh . . . tuh . . ."

70

Josh dropped the book on Mary's desk, turned to leave. He heard the recorder click off, then Mary's voice. "Josh."

He stopped, looked at her. "What's it all about?" she asked.

"I'm kuh . . . kuh . . . kuh . . . quit . . . quitting."

"Quitting?"

Josh nodded.

Mary stared at him. Slowly she rose, came to the other side of the desk.

Again, Josh started to leave. Mary took his arm. "Why?" she demanded.

Josh shrugged. He knew it didn't work. What good was therapy? When he needed it most, it blew up in his face; it all came apart.

"Tell me," Mary said.

"I cuh . . . cuh . . . can't." He looked away from her.

"You owe me that."

She took his arm, led him to the sofa.

He didn't want to hurt her feelings, tell her the therapy was worthless. But she pulled him down beside her.

"Okay, spill," she insisted.

"It's nuh . . . nuh . . . nuh . . . no good. Not yuh . . . yuh . . . your fault." He couldn't go on. For some dumb reason his eyes watered, he felt choked up. He blinked rapidly, held back the tears.

Mary sighed. "Josh, I know things are rough for you right now. Howie gone, your mother's divorce." Her voice grew softer. "All right, you've had a few failures. They can be awful. Believe me, I know. But you've made progress, you'll make more."

Josh couldn't trust himself to speak. He shook his head.

"Listen, Josh," Mary went on, "one day, when you're fluent, when your speech is easy, when you've really got a handle on it, you'll look back at today and be glad you kept going."

What a crock. What a pile of bull she's handing me, he thought.

"Josh?"

71

He had to answer her. She wasn't going to let him off the hook. Okay, then he'd tell her. "I duh . . . duh . . . don't believe you." By the wounded look on her face, he knew she was hurt. "I'm suh . . . suh . . . sorry."

The two locked stares. Mary's eyes dropped first. She got up, went to the window, looked out. Then she turned and faced him. "I've never lied to you, Josh. Have you ever known me to lie to you?"

"No, buh . . . buh . . . but it cuh . . . can't be duh . . . duh . . . done. I can't do . . . it. I'm hope . . . luh . . . luh . . . less."

Josh rose, went to the door. He turned to look at her. "Thu . . . thu . . . thanks for everything."

Mary reached out, then dropped her hands to her sides. Her face was pale. Was she trembling? He felt as if he had to say more, something to let her know he was grateful for what she had tried to do. She looked so . . . so defeated. But all he could manage was, "Well, so luh . . . luh . . . luh . . . long."

She took a step forward. "Just a minute. Before you go I want you to hear something."

She moved to the desk. "Come here," she said.

He hesitated. Why couldn't she just let him go and get it over with?

"Please, Josh."

He walked over, stood facing her before the desk. She leaned over, switched on the tape recorder. The girl's voice said, ". . . tuh . . . tuh . . . talking is tuh . . . tuh . . . tuh . . . terr . . . terrible for me. I cuh . . . cuh . . . cuh . . . can't. I can't duh . . . duh . . . duh . . ."

Josh shifted his weight uncomfortably. He wanted to get away from that thin, tortured voice. But Mary held her hand up, stopping him.

The voice on the recorder kept on. ". . . you're fuh . . . fuh . . . forcing me." Then the girl's voice broke into sobs.

Painfully, Josh listened, but he stood there under Mary's raised hand, her riveting gaze. Haltingly, backed up by sobs, the voice continued. "I'll neh . . . neh . . . never be able to duh . . . duh . . . duh . . . do it. Neh . . . neh . . . never . . ."

72

Mary stopped the recorder, dropped into her chair. "That was me, Josh," she said softly, almost in a whisper.

Bewildered, Josh looked at her. "You? On the tape?"

Mary sighed. "My stuttering was as bad as yours. Maybe worse."

Shaken, Josh sat down, stared at her. "I duh . . . duh . . . don't believe it."

"Believe it. I know just how you feel. I wanted to quit, too. And I did quit. For a whole year. The worst year of my life." She paused, then went on. "When I went back to therapy . . . no, when I crawled back to therapy I could hardly say a single word without stuttering. My own family couldn't understand what I said. I was falling apart, close to a nervous breakdown."

She sighed, remembering. Then she leaned over the desk. Her jaw was set, her eyes blazing. "I won't let you quit, Josh. It's as simple as that."

She clicked on the tape recorder. "December sixteenth," she said firmly. "Joshua Taylor."

Josh opened the book. He found the page. The words blurred through his tears.

But he cleared his throat and began to read.

Chapter Ten

The small shuttle plane dropped down below the peaks that cradled Winter Valley. The pilot turned to his passengers, some already dressed in ski clothes, and pointed ahead. The village could be seen at the bottom of the mountain. The pilot smiled. It had been a rough flight from Denver but he had made it safely and Josh noticed a discreet gratuity being slipped into the pilot's hand just before they landed. A folded fifty-dollar bill given with a soft "Thanks, Jim" by one of the regulars.

Josh looked down at Winter Valley. The gloom of the dull flight to Denver, sitting next to Jack Bender and listening to ski talk, was lifting a little. He was seated alone now in a single seat in the tail. Jack and his mother were up front near the pilot.

The little plane banked and headed for the airstrip about a mile from the village. Josh saw Jack talking animatedly with his mother, pointing to the big lift that climbed above the village. Josh sighed. Jack Bender was a miserable fact of life, an unfortunate happening that had to be accepted. But it wasn't easy.

The plane touched down gently. A bus from the village waited on the edge of the strip while the driver, dressed in a vaguely Alpine costume, ran up to unload the bags.

Josh saw Jack put a bill into the pilot's hand. He noticed that it was a twenty and he heard the pilot's soft "Thank you, sir." But the pilot's expression told Josh that Jack Bender was now probably being rated four on a scale of ten.

The bus turned into the long, straight road that approached the village. Snow was banked as high as the roof of the bus on either side of the road. Fresh, clean, powdery snow. Money-making snow that had fallen two days before their arrival.

Josh was not prepared for Winter Valley. Even the fancy pictures he had seen hadn't revealed the reality. This was Switzerland West, a movie set with live action. There was a feeling that cameras were hidden somewhere and that the director was waiting and the man with the clapper was going to say, "Alpine Village, take one."

The main street was filled with gaily bannered shops, restaurants, and bars, all festooned with scrolled woodwork and little balconies. A huge ice Santa with reindeer filled the square in front of the lodge. Christmas was certainly at home here. Even little bells on the horse-drawn sleighs, sixteen dollars a half-hour with driver, could be heard ringing everywhere.

And color. Myriad colors of ski costumes moving in and out of restaurants, bars, shops, moving joyfully, skis on shoulders, heading toward the slopes.

Josh followed Jack and his mother into the lodge. He sat in the huge lobby in front of the fire, waiting while Jack registered.

Jack came into the lobby with his big phony smile, throwing a key to Josh. "You're in number twelve, great view of the mountain. We'll be in number twenty, just down the hall. Go have fun and meet us for dinner at seven. Okay?"

Josh fingered the key. You didn't have to talk to Jack; he did the talking. Josh nodded.

He sat for a long time looking at the fire, trying to sort out his thoughts. Trying to think what he felt. Did he feel anything? So they had a room together, so what? So she's your mother. Big deal. So he could be your stepfather some day. That's the big deal! Josh felt a little sick. He gripped the key in his hand and stood up.

The room did have a view of the mountain. His duffle bag was on the luggage rack, the key to the ski locker was on the bureau. Josh closed the door. He didn't look out the window at the mountain; he looked at the notice on the back of the door. He read the whole thing, every word, including the price of the room, which was obscene. He knew his mother wasn't paying; he was the total prisoner of one Jack Bender. He plopped down on the bed and stared up at the ceiling. He had the rest of the afternoon to himself. He could try the slopes or he could just bum around, get oriented. He closed his eyes. When he woke up it was dark and time for dinner.

Jack Bender had three scotches before dinner and two on the way, and pretty soon he was exchanging laughs with the young couple at the next table and then the tables were shoved together and the four of them were yakking away as if they'd known each other forever.

Josh got up after dessert and only Sandra noticed. She kissed him goodnight and said they'd all be out on the slopes in the morning. Josh nodded and left.

He wandered into the lobby and flopped into a big chair near the fire. There were tables around the lobby and drinks were served to those who couldn't stand the noise and the desperate conviviality of the bar.

He ordered a Coke and signed the check with his room number. Jack had told him to sign for anything he wanted. Anything. Jack had laughed and nudged Sandra, who had failed to smile with her usual indulgence.

He sipped the Coke, studying the tables, looking at his watch. He sighed. He remembered the brochure for Winter Valley. "Five glorious days, four enchanting nights." So far, he wasn't enchanted.

Neither was the girl at the table on the other side of the fire. Well, not exactly a girl. A woman about twenty-two, twenty-three, around there. She was sitting at the table with another girl and there was this guy with them talking a blue streak to the other girl. It wasn't hard to guess that the guy had just met them and was looking for a little after-ski action. Pretty soon he got up from the table with the girl he'd been talking to. They made elaborate offers for the other one to come along with them on a tour of the night spots, but the other one, as though knowing the protocol, refused with a forgiving smile.

The two went off gaily and the other girl went back to

her drink, dropping her smile into the bottom of the tall, frosty glass.

Josh watched the little drama of acceptance and rejection and felt a jab of sympathy for the one abandoned. He thought she was a lot prettier than the other, but obviously she hadn't issued so open an invitation as her friend. Shy maybe. Josh considered smiling at her in a comradely way, but she got up and left the lobby.

Josh finished the Coke slowly, looked at his watch again. There was a floor plan of the lodge under the glass of his table. He saw that there was a game room down the hall from the lobby.

Nobody was in the game room. He picked a pinball machine and punched at it idly. The machine was irritating, refusing to let the ball score decently. He got mad at the machine and determined to outwit it. But he couldn't. Game after game, it still outplayed him.

Then he became aware of her. He didn't know how long she had been there but he heard the bell clanging on a nearby machine. It was the other girl, the rejected one.

Okay, he'd smile at her. But she didn't look up, just kept playing her machine, fighting it, making the bells clang in her mechanical victory.

They played there almost an hour, no sound but the pinball bells. He gave up the idea of smiling at her. And suddenly she was through. As she passed by him she smiled and said, "Good night."

Josh looked out of window of his darkened room. There was, indeed, a magnificent view of the mountain, lighted now by a brilliant moon. But he didn't need a mountain.

He thought of Lisa Schiller. This was the night of her party. He could just see Eddie Lenz running the party, handling Lisa as if he owned her.

Josh stayed at the window, undressing slowly. Down below in a wood-gated area was a large hot tub. Steam and laughter rose from the tub as a new couple came down the platform to the steps leading into the tub. Josh watched as the man dropped his robe and went down the steps. He was wearing very brief briefs. Then the girl dropped her robe and walked gracefully down the steps. She was wearing nothing.

Josh watched the girl swallowed up by the steam, heard the laughter as she slid into the water. Four nights of this. It wasn't going to be easy.

Then, as he was turning away from the window, he saw his mother and Jack Bender come down the platform to the top of the steps. Jack Bender dropped his robe. Josh pulled the drapes shut savagely. He heard words in his head that he had said once before. They're rotten! All the selfish, me-me, life-of-my own adults! All of them, rotten!

At five A.M. Josh heard the firing of the snow cannon. At the foot of the mountain the big, 105mm cannon was blasting into the heavy overhang of snow, releasing it into an artificial avalanche. Seasons back, skiers had been buried in avalanches, but now, in the days of big-money skiing, avalanches were created and tamed. With the fall of the snow, large Caterpillar tractors smoothed new trails in the now commercialized mountain.

Josh got up and opened the drapes. Nothing could stop the leap of joy at the sight of the mountain with the sun just coming over the top. He looked at it a long time, letting it reach out and touch him, invite him, present its untouched slopes to his eager skis.

He looked at his watch. The lifts didn't begin till nine. How could he wait that long? He dressed quickly. A run. He'd run in the hard-packed snow on the road leading out of the village. And that's what he did. As the sun warmed the mountain, Josh ran. He ran lightly, with joy, not feeling the thin air of the high altitude, just running to feel good. And looking up at the mountain on the way back, seeing himself on the slopes, he thought maybe it could be "five glorious days," after all.

Sandra's ski suit was a flowing one-piece, vivid blue. On the back of her jacket was a silver starburst, and the same starburst was repeated on the front of her skis. Jack Bender looked great on skis, Josh had to admit it. The guy had style, handled himself like a pro.

The three of them moved easily toward the lift. Josh's bindings weren't just right. He told them to go ahead, he'd meet them on the summit. He watched his mother move off with Jack. One thing, there wouldn't be a more beautiful skier on any slope than the lady with the starburst jacket. He noticed how the men coming downhill smiled at her. You couldn't blame them.

Josh stopped at the foot of the beginner's slope. He dropped to one knee to adjust his left binding. He didn't see anything, but he heard the wild yell of alarm. He turned just in time to get a flash of a figure, skis spread wide, ski poles flailing, bearing down on him at an uncontrollable speed.

The impact stunned him and Josh went down. The full weight of the flying figure piled on top of his left knee. In an instant he knew he was about to become an injury statistic.

The figure was a girl. The rejected girl from last night in the lounge and game room, and she was saying, "Are you hurt? Did I hurt you? Oh, I am so sorry!"

Josh's wind was partially knocked out so he couldn't say anything stupid like, "That's all right."

They untangled slowly and released their skis. The girl stood up. She held out her hand to Josh.

"I really am terribly sorry," she said. "I didn't know the things slid so fast. Are you all right?"

"Sh . . . sure, I'm fine," Josh lied. He tried to put down his left leg and fell clumsily back into the snow.

"Oh, dear," said the girl. "I really did mess you up."

A moment later a young man wearing a parka with the yellow cross of the ski patrol glided into the picture. He bent down to Josh.

"I'm all right," Josh said.

The young man smiled reassuringly. "Sure you are. But we'll just give you a ride back to the lodge." He pulled a hand radio out of his pocket and talked into it.

"Hey . . . luh . . . luh . . . look," Josh said, "I . . . I'm really okay." He tried to struggle to his feet.

"Now, please," the young man said, "just sit still."

Josh looked at the worried face of the girl who had run him down. He tried to smile, to show her it didn't hurt. But it did.

The girl sat down in the snow next to him. In spite of the pain he noticed that she was even prettier than he thought last night. And maybe younger. Twenty, twenty-one at the most.

The toboggan came up, pulled by two men of the rescue patrol. Josh felt ridiculous being put on the toboggan with everybody watching. As if he was such a lousy skier he couldn't get past the beginner's slope.

They towed him toward the infirmary which was housed in a separate wing of the lodge. The girl came along too, still offering variations of apology. Josh kept saying it was nothing.

The doctor looked at the knee, pushed it to see if it had slipped the socket, and listed Josh as a minor sprain. The doctor put an elastic brace on the knee and told Josh to quit skiing for a few days. Josh didn't explain that he hadn't been skiing at all.

The girl waited in the reception room. When Josh hobbled out she smiled in relief.

"You're going to live," she said.

Josh grinned. "I guess so."

"Oh, I'm so terribly . . ." she began.

Josh broke in. "It . . . it was my fault. I . . . I was in the way."

They laughed. "So you were," she said. "Here, put your arm around my shoulder. I'll be your crutch. Do you want to go to your room?"

He shook his head.

"How about a drink? No, you're too young, aren't you? They wouldn't serve you. Coffee?"

"I . . . uh . . . I'm not too young," Josh said. "I duh . . . don't drink in the morning."

She laughed again. "Okay, coffee."

They hobbled down the corridor that connected the infirmary with the main lodge.

"I shouldn't have put on skis in the first place," the

girl said. "It's just ridiculous, sliding down hills on a couple of slats at a hundred dollars a day."

Josh smiled, then winced as they negotiated a turn in the corridor.

"My name's Laurie," she said.

"Juh . . . Josh."

"Hi, Josh."

"I . . . I . . . huh . . . have a slight speech im . . . im . . . impediment," he stammered.

She smiled. "The rest of you okay?"

He laughed. "Far as I know."

He had never felt so easy with a girl. Maybe because she was older, more sophisticated. He couldn't have said that bit about the speech impediment to Lisa, or Vickie, or any of the others, but with this girl it seemed just the right way to go.

The steaming coffee tasted great. They were sitting outdoors on the sun terrace looking up at the mountain. They had exchanged where-you-froms—she was from San Francisco, worked for a newspaper there—and were getting into more relevant stuff.

"No, she's not my sister," Laurie said, referring to the other girl last night. "She works in my office at the newspaper. We cry on each other's shoulders."

"Wuh . . . wuh . . . what have you got to cry about?" he asked.

Laurie shrugged. "Enough. That's why I'm up here, getting away from it all."

"Oh," Josh said as if he understood.

They finished the coffee. Josh ordered them two more and the pastry tray. After all, Jack had said just sign the room number.

They dawdled for an hour, and Josh was wishing it could be more, when she said, "Look, I've loused up your skiing. Is there anything I could do . . ."

Josh said it without even thinking. "Luh . . . let's go for a sleigh ride this afternoon."

"Sleigh ride?"

"If . . . if you're not busy."

"Sleigh ride? With the horse, the jingle bells?"

81

"Wuh . . . wuh . . . would you?"

She leaned over, kissed his cheek and laughed. "I would, Joshua, I most certainly would love to go sleigh riding."

Chapter Eleven

Jack Bender was amused. He chuckled over his luncheon scotch when he heard that Josh had been clobbered on the beginner's slope. Sandra was not amused but accepted Josh's limp as the normal result of a skiing vacation.

Josh felt freed by his injury, since he wouldn't have to be with his mother and Jack on the slopes. He knew Jack would have given him skiing lessons and probably would have led him down one of the hairy runs to show him how it was done. On balance, the twisted knee might be a plus.

Laurie was waiting for him at the stable where the sleighs were rented. She looked fantastic in her bright red parka and cream-colored pants.

She ran up and took his arm as he limped toward her. She pointed to a sleigh with a large white horse. "That one! That's ours! Isn't he a darling?"

"The horse?" Josh asked.

"No, that wonderful man up front. Isn't he magnificent?"

The driver was a large man with a fierce mustache, a hawklike nose, and a wild, nameless fur coat.

"He's right out of Siberia," Laurie laughed. "You can almost hear the wolves following the sleigh."

Josh laughed. "Okay, that's the one."

They climbed into the sleigh, pulling the big buffalo robe over their knees.

The driver turned around and grinned, showing scraggly yellow teeth. "Where to, kids?" he said in an accent ten thousand miles from Siberia.

"You nah . . . nah . . . name it," Josh said. He gestured grandly in no particular direction. "Sh . . . show us the country."

"Yes, sir," the driver said. He slapped the reins on the horse's rump and they started off.

Josh had never been in a sleigh. The smooth, silent movement was like riding on air. Fabulous. They rode through the village street with bells jingling and people turning to smile at the pretty girl in the red parka and the slim, handsome young man at her side.

The driver turned to them. "My name is Eric," he said. He pointed to the horse. "Her name is Pansy."

Laurie laughed. "She's beautiful."

"She eats too much," said Eric, and slapped Pansy's rump with the reins.

They left the village and turned into a snow-banked road leading toward the back country.

Josh surrendered himself to the unbelievable present. The sensuous hiss of the runners on the hard-packed snow, the rhythmic jingle of the bells on the horse's collar, the last warmth of the sun beginning to sink behind the mountain, the green-and-white snow-covered hills. And this dazzling girl beside him, their shoulders touching, feeling silent pleasure from the touch.

They rode without talking, not daring to spoil a moment of it. Their mittened hands touched under the buffalo robe, and Josh took hers in his and held it.

They entered a grove of trees and the sudden cold drew them closer together. Eric turned with his scraggly grin. "You want coffee?" He nodded down the road. "Chalet coming up."

The chalet was the jumping-off place for the cross-country skiers and a regular stop for the sleighs.

On the far side of the trees they saw the steep-pitched roof of the chalet and a welcome plume of smoke coming out of the chimney.

They sat in a secluded booth, warming their hands around the coffee cups.

Laurie looked down at her steaming cup, then at Josh. "It's nice," she said.

"Yeah," Josh said. "Real nice."

"If we could only freeze the frame, like in the movies."

"Yeah," Josh sighed. "And ruh . . . roll the credits."

She laughed softly. " 'Wonderful Afternoon' created by Joshua. You deserve an Oscar."

He smiled. "Thu . . . thanks."

They sat for a moment not needing to speak. Then she said, "How old are you, Josh?"

"Suh . . . seventeen in February. Buh . . . basically, I'm thu . . . thirty."

She laughed. "Older man, huh?"

"Yeah."

She took a sip of her coffee, put it down slowly. "I'm twenty-three; I'm in the middle of a divorce. That's why I'm up here, to get it off my mind with skis."

Divorce. The word hit him. He thought of Howie and Bill and Sandra. Was it everybody? Every lousy couple in the world getting divorced, even this fantastic, wonderful girl sitting beside him. It was rotten, rotten, lousy. Why did they do it?

Laurie caught the anguished look on his face. "I'm sorry, I didn't mean . . ."

He shook his head. "No . . . no, it's all right." He called for the check.

They got back in the sleigh and it was suddenly colder. Josh pulled the robe over her and Eric clucked to Pansy.

The sleigh floated through the lengthening shadows. Josh suddenly put his arm boldly around Laurie's shoulder and drew her nearer. She turned her head to him. They kissed, holding each other closely, just for the moment . . .

Everybody was at the bar and the lounge was empty. After dinner, which Josh signed for with a lordly flourish, they sat in front of the fire, the big room all to themselves.

They were quiet for a long while, looking into the fire. Then Josh went on with the conversation that had been broken off at dinner.

"Huh . . . how did it happen?" Josh asked.

She shook her head. "I don't know, I really don't know. He just put down his wine glass after dinner one night and said he wanted a divorce."

Josh waited.

"I couldn't believe it. I thought he was kidding. We'd been married five years. I thought everything was beautiful. It was for me. But he said . . ."

Josh broke in. "Duh . . . different directions."

"What?"

Josh was remembering the night Sandra had made her statement. "He . . . he said you wuh . . . wuh . . . were growing in different directions."

She looked at him wide-eyed. "How did you know?"

Josh shrugged. "I . . . I guess that's what they all say."

"That *is* what he said. We'd grown apart. And before I could tell him we hadn't, that I loved him, that I'd do anything . . ." She stopped. "I sound like some awful soap opera, don't I?"

Josh smiled. "You want to cry, go ahead."

"I've done that," she said.

"Well, you want to guh . . . go someplace? Walk? A movie? There's a French comedy showing in the village."

"I'd prefer to just sit here a while." She put her hand over his. "Okay?"

So they sat there, hands touching. Josh felt very grown-up, very depressed, and very stirred inside. Grown-up because he was sitting holding hands with a twenty-three year old divorcée, depressed because her situation gave him a look into the bleak future of Sandra's divorce, the loss of Howie, and the desolate specter of Jack Bender. And stirred up inside because this fabulous, dazzling female was holding his hand and . . . and what? Did he dare imagine for one moment what sort of luscious body was hidden under the bulky ski clothes?

Laurie's girlfriend came bounding into the room, saying where on earth had Laurie been all day and being introduced to Josh and saying, "For heaven's sake come along; we've got a double date and we're going to the disco."

Laurie said, "Sorry . . ."

But her friend insisted, and then the two men came in and everybody was introduced, and Josh felt about ten years old and one of the guys said this terrific combo was playing and politely talked down to Josh, asking him along too but Josh politely refused and told Laurie to go ahead.

The girlfriend said, "You don't have to dress, Laurie. Let's go, okay? Time's wasting."

Laurie smiled. "Sorry, Josh and I are going to the French movie in the village."

The girlfriend looked stunned. She pointed to one of the men. "I told Eddie you'd . . ."

Laurie smiled at the one called Eddie. "Thanks, some other time, Eddie."

The girlfriend and the two men each gave Laurie a look of utter incredulity. Then they said goodnight and left.

All of a sudden Josh wasn't ten anymore. "You . . . you really want to go to the movie?"

"No, do you?"

"No."

They held hands in front of the fire and talked of what they'd do tomorrow. Later they had something to eat at the snack bar; then Josh walked her back to her room. His heart pounded, wondering whether she'd invite him in.

Then a noisy bunch of drunks came down the corridor and stopped to sing premature Christmas carols. Laurie kissed Josh fleetingly and closed the door.

Josh stood with his back pressed to the wall as the drunks stumbled by singing and calling out Merry Christmas. When they were gone he walked slowly back to his room, every corner of his mind and body touched by the wonder of Laurie. And he didn't even know her last name.

They were sitting at one of the tables around the skating rink. The skaters went by in a steady carousel of color and movement. Laurie sipped the strong, pungent tea and took large, wolfish bites of the rich chocolate pastry.

Josh didn't see the skaters; all he saw was Laurie sensuously smearing her face with chocolate. He knew, in the layer underneath fantasy, that nothing could come of all this. She was certainly, at his age, an "older woman." You couldn't get around that. And all this was happening because she was lonely and upset and needed someone to talk to. Anyone.

She licked a chocolate flake off her upper lip, smiled at him. "You're a very nice guy, Josh."

He returned the smile.

"I'll bet your brother misses you," she said.

He had told her about Howie.

"I . . . I miss him," Josh said.

Laurie nodded.

They watched the skaters a moment. "If Chuck were here, right this minute, sitting right there . . ."

She had told him about Chuck, her soon-to-be ex-husband. "I'd say . . ." She hesitated.

Josh waited as if what she was going to say was very important, as if his whole life hung on the sentence.

"I'd say, Chuck, you are a louse, a complete, total, no-good louse."

"Buh . . . but you love him," Josh added.

She bit off the last piece of chocolate, chewed thoughtfully. "Maybe, I don't know." She dabbed at her lips with the paper napkin. "I think I'm addicted to chocolate. Did you know that people could get hung up on chocolate?"

What he knew was that he was hung up on her and that his vacation could last no more than five days and that two were almost gone and once they left Winter Valley that would be the end of it.

"Yeah . . . I nuh . . . know that," Josh said. "People can get hung up on anything."

"Like you and me," she laughed.

He was startled that she had read him so well. He tried not to show it. "Yeah," he said. "Kup . . . couple of losers."

"Uh-uh," she said firmly. "Finders." She put her hand over his. "We're finders, Josh. Right?"

He nodded, unable to put anything into words.

The waiter came by pushing the pastry tray. Josh raised his hand, stopping him.

"No," Laurie objected. "I couldn't, really."

The waiter knew his craft. He waited.

"Well," Laurie said, "just that little one there."

The waiter put the small chocolate cream on her plate and moved on.

Josh watched her bite into the chocolate cream. She held out the other half; he shook his head.

They watched the skaters a while and then, as if at an inner signal, they got up and left the table. They walked out of the rink onto the snow path toward the lodge.

Laurie held his arm, pressing close to him.

"Would anyone be in your room?" she asked.

"Nuh . . . no, I'm alone."

"Let's go there and just talk some more."

They entered the lodge. People were coming in from skiing, heading for the bar. Nobody noticed them as they went across the lobby and down the corridor to room twelve.

Josh closed the door. His heart was pounding. She threw her ski coat into one chair and plopped herself into another one.

They stayed there and talked, their chairs pulled close together, their hands touching now and then. It was dark before they realized it, and the view of the mountain was breathtakingly clear in the moonlight.

Laurie gazed out of the picture window. "Isn't it beautiful?"

"Yeah," Josh said, gazing at her profile outlined against the light of the moon. "Beautiful."

There was silence for a moment. Then: "Hey, aren't we hungry?" Laurie said.

"I guess so," Josh answered.

"What time is it?"

Josh got up and switched on the lamp; he looked at

his watch. "Almost eight. We . . . kuh . . . kuh . . . could eat here in the room."

She laughed. "In bed?"

He looked at her to see if she were joking. He couldn't tell. "Uh . . . anything you say."

"I say I love you, Josh."

She couldn't mean it, of course. He could mean it. But how could she?

She looked at him tenderly. "Steak. I'd like a steak, medium rare."

Could she? Mean it?

"And maybe a bottle of nice burgundy."

He picked up the phone before she could say she was only kidding, and asked for room service.

They had the dinner served on the table in front of the window, looking up at the mountain.

The lights were on at the lower slopes. The skiers came down from the shadows and moved into the light, gliding silently on the fluffy snow.

Josh knew he would always remember their lovely time together.

After dinner was over they sat silently a long while and then she kissed him on the cheek and said, simply, "Thank you, Josh."

In the morning, he stretched out in bed, smiled, rolled over luxuriously, and looked at his watch. He wondered now what time it was when she'd gone back to her own room. He could still catch a faint trace of her perfume in the room here, still feel the closeness, the tenderness, the crazy, wild delight he had shared with her.

And how simple, how natural, how perfect it had been. She accepted him for what he was, stuttering and all. No reservations, no holding back, no playing emotional games.

Perfect.

He leaned over to the nightstand and picked up the phone. He'd call her room, tell her how he felt. He didn't realize that he had lifted the phone without fear, commanded the monster without even thinking.

"Laurie Farley's room, please. I thu . . . think, it's number sixty."

The desk clerk's voice came back in a moment. "I'm sorry, sir, Mrs. Farley checked out this morning."

Josh held the phone numbly. "Are you sure?"

"Quite sure," said the clerk's voice. "She checked out about eight o'clock."

"Uh . . . thu . . . thank you," Josh said.

He put down the phone slowly, got out of bed. His stomach had tightened into a painful knot. Trancelike, he moved toward the bathroom, wondering whether he was actually going to be sick.

On the way back, he saw her note, slipped under the door. He picked it up. Her handwriting was large, generous, forthright. The big letters seemed loving, tender, understanding. The note said: "Let's always be finders, Josh. Let's always remember each other with love. Laurie."

He read it over and over. He put it on the table in front of the window and read it again and again while dressing. Then he put the note in his shirt pocket.

The note stayed in his pocket for his remaining days at Winter Valley. His knee got better but he didn't ski. He took walks in the woods and thought about Laurie. It even crossed his mind to ask the clerk where she lived and call her. But he knew it was better the way she had left it. And he had the note in his pocket. He'd always have that.

On the last day, his mother called his room and said they'd all have breakfast together.

Jack Bender was alone at the table when Josh sat down.

"Hi," said Josh.

Jack looked up from the piece of paper on his plate. He stared coldly at Josh, not answering the hi. He picked up the piece of paper. Josh could see it was the bill from the lodge, with a long list of entries.

"How come you racked up fifty-five dollars for room service?" Jack asked.

Josh was too surprised to answer.

"Or is it a mistake?"

Josh shook his head.

"Fifty-five dollars. For what?"

"Duh . . . dinner," Josh stuttered.

"Duh . . . dinner," Jack mimicked. "You ate fifty-five dollars worth of dinner? You and who else?"

Josh could barely get it out. "A . . . a . . . fuh . . . fuh . . . friend."

Jack looked down at the bill. "And thirty-five bucks sleigh riding. With a friend, huh?"

Josh nodded. Then: "You . . . you tuh . . . told me to sign fuh . . . fuh . . . for anything I wanted."

"Yeah, I did. But I didn't tell you to spend my money on some little tart you picked up."

Josh grabbed the table, held on for control.

"Oh, don't think your mother and I didn't notice what was going on. I asked at the desk who she was. I nosed around." He looked at Josh contemptuously. "A divorcée, from Frisco no less. And on the make for a sixteen-year-old kid."

Josh jumped up, his face red with rage. Other diners turned around. Josh didn't care. "You . . . chu . . . cheapskate!" he yelled, and grasped the edge of the table to keep from striking out at Jack as Sandra ran into the dining room.

Jack just stared back, as though acutely aware of the embarrassing squabble he had created.

Sandra jerked Josh away. He turned to his mother with a look of fury and ran out of the room.

Sandra sat down, breathing hard, plainly upset. The eyes of the other diners turned away reluctantly, deprived of a diverting moment. Sandra looked at Jack angrily. "What did you say to him?"

Jack shrugged. "I didn't say anything. He's just a touchy kid." Jack folded the bill and slipped it into his pocket. He put a smile back on his face, looked at the other diners as if to assure them that it had been nothing. He turned back to Sandra. "How about Eggs Benedict?"

"What did you say to him, Jack?"

"Nothing. Nothing at all. The kid just doesn't like me this morning." He grinned. "I think he's jealous."

Sandra kept looking at him. Jack lowered his eyes. "Well," he asked, "are you going to eat?"

"All right," said Sandra. She looked at the menu hungrily. "I'll have the Eggs Benedict."

The big 747 dropped lower for its final approach. Josh, alone at a window seat, looked down on the dirt-brown floor of the Mojave Desert. They were almost home. He touched the shirt pocket where the note from Laurie was hidden. At the last minute he had obtained her address from the clerk at the lodge and spent much time writing wonderful letters to her in his head. And now, on the plane, he was thinking out the final unwritten letter. He rejected the ships-that-pass-in-the-night angle, but he knew that's what it was. He wouldn't ever see her again. Oh, maybe years from now when they were both married, or he was traveling in Greece on an archeological mission. He had found a book on archeology at the lodge when he was bored with TV. Archeology seemed like a good enough way to go.

Anyway, they'd meet on the island of Noxos in the Aegean Sea and she'd hardly recognize him because he'd have this gorgeous black beard, but finally she'd yell "Joshua!" and he'd take her in his arms . . .

"Seatbelts, please," the stewardess said, tapping his shoulder.

"Oh . . . sorry," said Josh. He hadn't noticed the flashing sign. He fastened the belt and never got back to Greece because at that moment Jack Bender, sitting two seats ahead, turned around with his stuck-on smile and gave Josh a thumbs-up gesture, for what Josh couldn't figure out except that Jack had been playing it very low key since the row at breakfast and was probably trying to smooth things over with Sandra. And since Jack hadn't said anything to his mother, Josh hadn't said anything either. But Josh looked back at Jack, who was grinning and holding his thumb up, and thought the guy was really a terrible con artist.

Chapter Twelve

Carmela welcomed them back, and the wonderful news was that Bill had called and was driving down with Howie, and Howie was going to stay with them for Christmas and maybe even a couple of days after.

Josh thought of his terrific present for Howie, the rocket he'd bought with his own money, and he could hardly wait to see Howie's face when he opened the box.

The next two days inched by, and then he saw Bill's car coming in the driveway, Howie jumping out before the car even stopped. Josh went to meet him.

Howie rushed up and whacked him, and he walloped Howie and they wrestled around and said each other's names, and Sandra came out and kissed Howie and kissed Bill, and Bill shook Josh's hand. Then Carmela came out and Howie ran to her and hugged her, and it was a bloody miracle that nobody cried, and they all went back in the house carrying Howie's duffle bag and other junk.

When it all calmed down, Josh and Howie went back to their bedroom.

Howie threw his duffle bag on the lower bunk, sat down, and exhaled loudly.

Josh sat down. They looked at each other, smiled.

"How you been?" Howie asked.

"Okay," said Josh. "How you been?"

"Okay."

"How's it going at Skytop?"

"Okay. We go skiing."

"Good."

"School stinks. Two guys run everything. One guy is

named Hinkle. I get to fight him practically every day. Did you ski at Winter Valley?"

"No. This girl, she came down the beginner's slope and ran into me and knocked my knee out. Actually, she wasn't a girl. She was a married woman."

Howie nodded. "They fall a lot."

"Well, she was a young married woman."

Howie caught a note of mystery. "Hey, you scored!"

Josh grinned. "Where'd you get this 'scored' business?"

"Did you? Score?"

"You're too young to . . ."

"You scored," Howie said.

Josh whacked Howie on the shoulder. "You're a smart-aleck, know that?"

"Yeah, that's what Hinkle says. Hey, did Bill tell you? I get to stay here till two days after Christmas. Maybe we'll have a flood in Somerville Canyon. Wouldn't that be terrific?"

Josh laughed. "The cops could bring us home."

"With a white cat. Hey, I was thinking, Josh, on the way down. Maybe I could get sick and stay longer . . . through New Year's. Chicken pox, maybe?"

Josh laughed. "You already had chicken pox."

"Remember when I gave them to you?"

Josh nodded.

"Listen," said Howie. "Where are all the records? We could work the hi-fi."

"I broke them getting mad at Jack Bender."

"You hit him with the records?"

"I wish I had."

Howie gave Josh a sidelong glance. "That thing still going with him and your mother?"

"Bad as ever," said Josh.

"Maybe he'll drop dead."

"No way. He's too mean to do anybody a favor."

Howie got up from the bunk, untied the string on his duffle bag. "I take my bunk?"

"Sure."

Howie unzipped the duffle bag, brought out a box. "For Carmela."

"What is it?"

"Don't you remember. The manager scene, this guy made it."

"Oh yeah, hide it."

Howie pulled out another box. "And this is for you."

"What's in it?"

"Horse manure."

"Just what I wanted," said Josh.

"But you can't open it till Christmas."

And a last box. "This is for Sandra. Bill helped me pick it out."

"She'll love it," said Josh.

"You don't know what's in it."

"Perfume."

"How'd you know?"

"I'm five years older than you."

Howie grinned. The last thing he pulled out was a new science fiction magazine. He handed it to Josh.

"You still into space?" Josh asked.

"Yeah." He smiled. "I just brought it along in case I couldn't sleep."

Josh knew the whole thing was phony but he couldn't help enjoying it. Here they were, the four of them, Sandra, Bill, Howie, and Josh decorating the tree on Christmas Eve just as they had always done. Just as if Sandra and Bill weren't in the middle of a divorce, Sandra laughing and Bill making jokes and all of them bouncing around like kids as the familiar ornaments came out of the boxes and were hung on the tree.

But the really ridiculous part was Sandra and Bill going to this party afterward. The same party they went to every year, given by the same people who loaned them their house in Palm Springs when Sandra and Bill were married. And now, here was Bill staying in a motel and all of them pretending it was like it used to be.

Sandra took the silver star out of the box and handed it to Howie. Bill lifted Howie up, and Howie put the star on the top of the tree. Then they all cheered and Josh turned on the lights. Bill turned on the stereo, caught a Christmas carol, and Sandra got all misty-eyed and hugged Josh and then Howie. And when Bill held out his arms she hugged him too. How stupid can you get? But it was Christmas, and at nine o'clock Sandra and Bill rushed off to the party.

Josh and Howie sat down at the foot of the tree where the unopened presents lay in silent promise.

Howie listened as the car went out the driveway. After a moment he said: "Josh . . . do you think . . ."

"Uh-uh," said Josh. "Not a chance."

"But he kissed her and . . ."

"No way," said Josh. "They're being civilized."

"But he still likes her, I know he does."

"So?" Josh asked.

"So, maybe . . ."

"Howie, you heard them that night. They've grown in different directions."

"That's a lot of bull-pucky."

"Sure it is. But they want something new."

"What about us?"

"You tell me."

Howie sighed. "Let's open the presents."

"Not till morning."

Howie looked at the long box with the tag that said: "For my brother."

"I'll bet it's a rocket," Howie said.

"It's a used athletic supporter from the Rams' locker room."

Howie grinned. "Gee, Josh, how did you know?" He looked at the tree. "They grow wild at Skytop."

Josh got up from the floor, surveyed the tree. "Well, at least the tree is real."

Howie got up. "Yeah, and it smells good. Like camp, like getting lost in the woods."

Josh laughed. "Yeah, just like camp." He yelled toward the kitchen. "Carmela!"

"Did you tell her to put real booze in the eggnog?" asked Howie.

"Sure."

"Carmela!" Howie yelled.

"Come on," said Josh.

They ran into the kitchen. Carmela was holding a

teaspoon under a bottle of brandy. Josh got a tablespoon out of the drawer and handed it to her.

Carmela sighed in mock resignation and poured two tablespoons of brandy into each eggnog.

They sat at the kitchen table just as they had done every year after Sandra and Bill went off to the party. And they raised their eggnogs in a quiet toast and drank.

Howie ran his tongue around his lips to lick off the creamy yellow fuzz.

"Feliz navidad," said Josh.

"Feliz navidad," Howie said.

"Merry Christmas," said Carmela, and tears began rolling down her cheeks.

"Aw, Carmela, cut it out," Josh said.

"She always cries on Christmas," said Howie.

"I know, I know."

"It's because she's so happy. Right, Carmela?"

Carmela nodded.

"And she's going to seven o'clock mass in the morning. Right, Carmela?" Josh said. He banged his mug on the table. "And we're going with her."

Howie looked dumbfounded. "We're what?"

"We're going to mass, Carmela. With you."

"Josh . . . that's seven o'clock," said Howie.

"We're going."

"The presents."

"We'll open them when we come back. Okay, Carmela?"

Carmela sobbed joyfully and kissed Howie.

"Hey, it's his idea," Howie said.

She kissed Josh, then ran off to her room, presumably for a handkerchief to stem the flow of joy.

"You got her all worked up," Howie said.

Josh nodded. "We never did this before. We should've."

"But seven o'clock. And all that singing and praying."

"Do you good."

"Guess so," Howie nodded. "We could pray, too. Maybe Jack Bender would drop dead."

"It's an angle," said Josh.

They sipped their eggnogs thoughtfully. Howie licked

the fuzz off his lips again. "There's a kid up in Skytop; he's twelve; he's an alcoholic."

"Happens," said Josh.

Howie downed the rest of his eggnog. "Well, what the heck. Merry Christmas."

"The same," said Josh and downed the rest of his eggnog.

The terrific part about going to mass with Carmela was that Josh got to drive Sandra's second car. It was a clunky old Mercedes with about half as much guts as a used Pinto, but it was still a Mercedes, and if you lived in the Canyon you had to have at least one for status.

At six-forty-five in the morning there was hardly a car on Sunset. Josh rounded the many curves skillfully and only Carmela, in the back seat, was unaware that they were taking the dangerous "S" curves in Watkins Glen and piling up points for top driver of the year. Howie knew.

"Come on, chicken," said Howie softly. "Stomp on this thing."

Josh grinned, pressed down the accelerator. The old crate, tires protesting, lumbered around a turn.

"Tan rapido!" Carmela said in alarm.

Josh laughed, thinking "too fast" sounded the same in any language.

The church was in Brentwood, only a few miles from home. In the parking lot, Carmela waited while Josh locked the car, then walked with quiet pride between her boys.

A neighbor from the Canyon saw Carmela and called out, "Good morning, Carmela."

Carmela returned the greeting. Howie smiled at the neighbor and took Carmela's hand to show that he was indeed one of her boys. Josh offered his arm and Carmela took it, letting him lead her into the church.

The organ was playing "Silent Night" as they entered; Carmela knelt to the altar, then led them into a pew.

The church was alive with pageant and color for Christmas. On one side of the altar was a crèche, a beautiful tableau of precious carved figures displaying

99

the stable at Bethlehem. The already risen sun was lighting the stained-glass window, bringing alive the saints, who looked down with unremitting compassion on the congregation below.

It was bewildering, exciting and mysterious to Josh and Howie. They knelt when Carmela knelt, stood up when she stood up, felt a tingle of drama when the priest came to the altar arrayed in a blaze of gold and white.

"The grace of our Lord, Jesus Christ, and the love of God and the fellowship of the Holy Spirit be with you all," the priest said in awesome tones through the hidden loudspeaker.

"And also with you," the congregation responded.

"Lord, have mercy."

"Christ, have mercy."

It was beautiful, mysterious. But somewhere along the line Josh got to thinking about other things. About him and Howie. Was this the end of the line? Would there be only brief meetings on holidays, summers maybe, but gradually drifting away, gradually living separate lives? Was this the way it was going to be?

He looked at Howie, now kneeling with Carmela, and he felt an almost painful, protective tenderness toward his brother.

The congregation was singing "Oh, Come, All Ye Faithful."

And then, before he came back to reality, the mass was nearly over. Josh and Howie waited while Carmela went up to the altar for communion.

Josh stared at her and glanced at Howie. The boy's eyes were shining as he, too, followed Carmela's movements. Josh knew that next year, if there was a next year, the three of them would be here together again.

Driving back, Josh had the peculiar feeling of being up and down at the same time. And Howie was uncharacteristically subdued. Maybe he, too, was thinking into an uncertain future.

But then they got home with unscraped fenders and ran into the house. And under the tree were all the presents.

Howie was ready to pounce upon them, but Josh made him wait until they presented Carmela with their gift. This time she had her handkerchief ready for the tears. And then she gave each of the boys a translucent, colorful Saint Christopher medal and watched with joy as Howie exclaimed over his "good luck charm" and Josh tucked his medal carefully into his wallet.

Then the boys dropped down and began tearing off the wrappings of other gifts, and when Howie saw his rocket and Josh saw the terrific pair of Nike running shoes that Howie had given him, they knew finally that this was something real, certain, concrete and immutable: Christmas presents. This, at least, was back just as it used to be.

Howie looked joyfully at his rocket. "Hey," he said grinning at Josh, "let's go out and blow us up to the moon."

Chapter Thirteen

The day after Christmas, they took a hike up Somerville Canyon. The raging river that had torn through the canyon years before was now a quiet little stream alongside the new road.

They stood for a while on the bank, tossing leaves into the moving water, watching as the leaves floated downstream and out of sight.

"The sofa," said Josh. "Remember the sofa?"

"Yeah," Howie said.

"I wonder what ever happened to that sofa."

"And the cat," Howie added. "That sure was one dumb cat."

"And one dumb kid brother," Josh smiled.

Howie sighed. "Yeah, pretty dumb."

They moved on, away from the stream and out onto the road.

"Josh . . ."

"Yeah?"

"You know all about girls, don't you?"

"Yeah," said Josh. "Everything."

"I mean, no kidding."

"All right, half of everything."

"There's this girl in my class," said Howie. "Lizzie."

Josh felt an almost imperceptible stab of jealousy.

"She's a pain in the rear," said Howie.

Josh felt better.

". . . but she keeps asking me to come to her house. She says she's got a hot tub. Is that a come-on, Josh?"

Josh smiled. "What do you think?"

"I think she's on the make. What do I do?"

Suddenly Josh thought back to the hot tub in Winter Valley, the vivid picture of his mother and Jack Bender.

"Keep out of hot tubs," said Josh curtly.

Howie looked up in surprise. "Why? Maybe I could score like you did."

"Stop talking like a stupid kid," Josh said harshly.

"Okay, okay," Howie said not knowing how he had offended. "All I said was . . ."

"Forget it," said Josh. He disliked himself for letting his feelings out on Howie. They walked along a minute in awkward silence.

"How are your legs?" Josh asked.

"Huh?"

"Could you run all the way home?"

"I can if you can."

"Okay, let's go."

They jogged easily down the road side by side, Howie matching steps with his brother, and once they were into it, a mile or so, they felt better.

"Josh . . ."

"Yeah?"

"Could we be together this summer, you think?"

"We got to be together," said Josh.

"Yeah," Howie said. "All summer. You could come to Skytop."

"Or you could come here."

Howie grinned up at Josh. "You could come to Skytop and take Lizzie off my hands."

Josh chuckled. "Okay."

"Break her in, kind of."

Josh laughed. "You're getting to be an awful smart-mouth, aren't you?"

"Yeah, that's what Bill says."

They ran comfortably down the road feeling close, in tune, their light sneakers sounding the steps together.

Bill's car stopped in the driveway. He turned off the lights and sat a moment, thinking, running it over in his mind. Was he really firm on this? Was it the right way to go?

Sandra had sounded a little wary over the phone

when he said he'd like to come over and talk a few minutes. She had a date with that Jack character, but he said he'd only stay a few minutes and it was important.

Bill could see the lights in the boys' room. Howie would be packing so they could leave first thing in the morning. Maybe his timing wasn't right, maybe he should write her a long letter. Ah, might as well go do it now, one time is as bad as the next.

Howie and Josh greeted him, and Howie said he was almost packed and could they please stay an extra day anyway and Bill laughed and said they'd be leaving in the morning.

Then Sandra came in looking absolutely smashing in a new outfit. Bill wanted to say let's call off the lawyers, but he didn't. He gave her an ex-husbandly hug and told Howie to go back and finish packing and Josh to help him because he and Sandra wanted to talk a little business.

The boys went back to their room. A little business was always divorce stuff.

But it wasn't divorce stuff.

Bill sat down in the big chair opposite Sandra's desk. She had turned the den into a home office, a retreat from the rest of the house.

A tray was waiting with two cups of coffee. She handed one to Bill.

He sipped his coffee, looking at her over the rim of the cup.

"You said it was important," Sandra began.

"Yeah. Yeah, I did."

"If it's about the community settlement . . ."

Bill shook his head. "Uh-uh, not business tonight."

She waited. He put down his coffee cup.

"Kids, Sandra. It's about kids. Josh and Howie."

"Oh," Sandra said. "Kids."

"Yeah. It's . . . it's good to see them together," said Bill. "They get along so well. Like . . . well, like they were real brothers, know what I mean?"

"Yes, they do get along."

"So I've been thinking. I mean, I've given this a lot of

thought, Sandra. It's not like a sudden idea or anything . . ."

Sandra looked at her watch.

"Okay, okay, I'll put it on the table."

"Please do."

"Well . . ." Bill smiled. He hoped he was smiling winningly. "Well, what I was thinking, Sandra, these boys ought to be together. Not just holidays or weekends, really together, know what I mean?"

"No, I don't know what you mean."

Bill shook his head. "I'm lousy at explaining things."

"I'll go along with that."

"Okay," Bill said sitting up straight. "Okay, here's the bottom line."

"I do dislike that meaningless phrase, *bottom line*. Just say what you want to say, Bill."

"All right, I want to say this. I want to take Josh on, have him live with us."

"Take him on?"

"Adopt him. Now look, Sandra, I know that sounds out of the ball park . . ."

"Must you say *out of the ball park* and *bottom line?* Haven't you got any words of your own?"

"Come off it, why do you get so superior when . . ."

"When you make an absurd proposal to adopt my son!"

"What's absurd? Those two kids . . ."

"Never mind those two kids, I'm talking about my son, Joshua. How do you dare . . ."

"Look," said Bill, getting as angry as she. "The kids need each other!"

"What are you implying? That I'm an unfit mother?"

Bill slammed his fist on the desk. "Stop it! Don't talk like that!"

Sandra took a deep breath, as though she were off the hook for a moment. "Okay," she said.

Bill was seething. "Those boys belong together! Josh needs a home!"

"And what does he have here?"

"He has Carmela! That's all he has! When are you around?"

"Now, look . . ."

"You look!" said Bill, hotly. "I told you I thought this thing out! It's my fault as much as yours. All we ever did was go out to parties, weekends, traveling around, you name it, anything but give them a little time!"

"Josh is not up for adoption, Bill."

"Sandra, you don't have to put it like that, as if I'm trying to buy him."

"How do you want me to put it? You're proposing to take my son . . ."

"When do you ever see him? You're bouncing around from one guy to the next . . ."

"Bouncing!" Sandra yelled. "I like that. I really like that!"

"Well, aren't you? After this jerk Bender there'll be another one . . ."

Sandra stood up. "I'm expecting company any minute."

". . . and after him, someone else. You'll never come to rest, Sandra, you'll always be looking for someone, just like you did when we were together."

She started toward the door. He stepped in front of her. "It's the truth. You were always looking. Al Kelton, what's-his-name, the golf pro . . ."

Sandra glared at him coldly. "I have company coming, Bill."

". . . and Johnny Stearns."

"At least Johnny Stearns was interesting, spontaneous, he did something besides nurse a ticker tape."

"You'll never settle down, Sandra."

"Not with mediocrity. No, I won't."

Bill sighed heavily. Now he looked at his watch. "I'll take Howie tonight, no use waiting till morning."

"Suit yourself."

"Sandra, what are we fighting about? All I want . . ."

"All you want is Joshua, and you can't have him. Clear?"

"It would be best for both of them."

"The bottom line?" she said acidly.

He sighed again. "Okay, go meet your company, Sandra. I'll get Howie."

106

Bill left Sandra's office and went down the hall to the boys' bedroom. Howie was stuffing the last sneaker into the duffle bag. He saw the strained look on Bill's face.

"Hi, Dad. Almost packed."

Bill came into the room. Josh was wrapping Howie's rocket in its original box. Bill ruffled Josh's hair affectionately.

"Change of plans, Howie. We're going tonight."

"Tonight!" Howie wailed. "You said till *two* days after Christmas."

"I'll explain it in the car." He pointed to his watch. "You've got five minutes. So long, Josh. We'll be in touch."

Josh nodded slowly, knowing it wasn't the time to ask questions.

Bill left the room. They could hear him go into the kitchen and say something to Carmela.

Dismally, Howie looked at Josh. "Must've been more than just a little business."

"Yeah," said Josh. "It must've been a real killer."

"Yeah."

Chapter Fourteen

It was downhill all the way after Howie and Bill left. Josh almost wore out the new running shoes, pounding along the roads at dawn, running endlessly in a nowhere journey down the beach, burning up the loneliness, running away from the void of Howie's abrupt departure.

Then came New Year's Eve. He dreaded it. His mother and Jack were giving a "small party for a few close friends." He knew what that would mean, twenty or thirty noisy drunks, himself dragged into it, the chic, laughing women pawing him: "My, how he's grown." "Ohhh, he's so handsome." And the men: "Who do you like in the Bowl, Josh?" "You into basketball this year, Josh?" And he'd have to answer. His mother's eye would be on him even while she was laughing with someone and she'd expect him to answer the questions and not stutter, embarrass her. He dreaded it.

After the party started, he slipped off and walked to the village to the movie. The Little Cinema was showing two reruns, one about a colony of giant grasshoppers that invaded New York and almost destroyed it, and the other about a cop who ratted on his buddies and lost the respect of his wife and kids but managed to make out with the girl reporter.

There weren't more than twenty-five people in the theater; twenty-five people who had nothing to do on New Year's Eve. During the intermission when the management hoped to sell a little popcorn, Josh saw Dudley Weiner sitting a few rows in front of him, biting aggressively into a giant caramel fudge bar.

Dudley Weiner was in Josh's class. He was forty pounds overweight, had squinty eyes and few friends

108

but lots of money and his own car, a new MG roadster. Dudley's father was a theatrical lawyer who made fabulous movie deals that shortchanged all the creative talent but left him and the producer with plently of after-tax goodies.

Josh thought of saying hello to Dudley and sitting next to him, but the second feature started before he could yield to the impulse.

Josh sat numbly through the agonies of the cop who was ratting on his buddies and heading for the arms of the girl reporter. Awful stuff, but he wanted to be anywhere but at his mother's party.

He sat through the cop flick and the last showing of the grasshopper movie. When the lights went up he and Dudley were the only ones left in the theater.

Dudley got up and ambled up the aisle, unwrapping another caramel fudge bar. He saw Josh, smiled.

"Hi," Dudley said.

Josh joined Dudley in the aisle. "Hi," Josh answered.

"Some grasshoppers, huh?" Dudley said.

"Yeah, lots of guh . . . grasshoppers."

They went past the closed candy counter and out the front door. They stood under the marquee a moment.

"Where's your car?" Dudley said.

"I walked."

"You walked?" said Dudley skeptically.

"Yeah."

Dudley looked at his Seiko, quartz-accurate-to-within-ten-seconds-a-month wristwatch. "Hey, only twenty-five minutes till New Year's.

Josh nodded.

"You want a ride home?" Dudley asked.

Josh shook his head. "Party at my house."

Dudley understood immediately. "Mine, too. My sister. My folks are away and she's got a lot of hot-shots from her college. They're going to tear the place down." He held out the fudge bar. "Candy?"

"No, thanks."

"Okay," said Dudley, "be seeing you." He ambled slowly toward his car, the last one left in the parking lot.

Josh thought again of the party at his house, the noise,

109

the drunken laughter, the chic ladies: "Ohhh, isn't he *adorable!*"

"Hey, Dudley . . ."

Josh caught up with Dudley. "Chu . . . changed my mind. Okay?"

"Hop in," said Dudley.

The little MG burbled into life and swung into the boulevard. Dudley always kept the top down, but the night was mild and the air felt good.

Dudley's house was only one canyon away from Josh's. Already Josh could see himself jogging home, or maybe taking a long run, burning up the time, maybe staying out all night. They wouldn't miss him.

Dudley went in through the kitchen and led Josh upstairs to his room. Two giant speakers were blasting out over the swimming pool. Josh could feel the deep bass thump that was probably assaulting neighbors for miles around.

From Dudley's room they looked down on the pool. The lights were low but bodies could be seen, apparently dancing. There were shouts and laughter and the sound of a glass breaking on the slate decking.

They turned away from the window. Dudley looked at his watch. "Ten minutes to go."

Josh nodded.

Dudley opened the door of the room, looked downstairs. "Wait," he said, and went out of the room. He was back quickly holding two glasses and a large cutglass decanter with a dark brown liqueur. He set the glasses down on his desk, opened the top of the decanter, sniffed it. "This is all I could get. He held it out to Josh. "Know what it is?" Dudley asked.

Josh sniffed the top of the decanter. "You got me. Don't you?"

"Uh-uh." Dudley poured a little of the liquid into a glass, tasted it. "Mmm, not bad." He poured some into the other glass, handed it to Josh.

Josh hesitated a second. He wasn't much into the booze scene. He'd had wine from time to time and leftover cocktails at some of his mother's parties, but he didn't particularly go for the stuff.

110

"Come on," said Dudley.

Well, what the heck, it *was* New Year's Eve. Josh sipped the sweetish, heavy liqueur. It did taste good, like liquid candy. And it was warm going down. He could feel the delicious heat all the way.

Dudley swept his lips with a sticky tongue. "Hey, not bad at all."

Josh took another, more aggressive sip. Yes, it really was good. He'd never had anything like this before. He took a third sip, rolled the heady stuff around on his tongue, then let it slide down in another wave of delightful warmth.

Dudley raised the decanter. Josh held out his glass. Dudley didn't know how much to pour. A half-glass seemed reasonable and after all, it was a big decanter.

Josh was beginning to feel a little more relaxed about New Year's Eve. He smiled at Dudley, held up his glass at Dudley.

"Yeah, not bad," Dudley said.

In school Dudley was not known as a brilliant conversationalist, but Josh didn't mind. This was friendly, laid back, kind of.

Dudley took a large swallow, exhaled with satisfaction. "My sister is a jerk," he said.

Josh nodded sagely. "My . . . muh . . . mother's buh . . . boyfriend is one too."

"Lotsa jerks in the world," Dudley philosophized.

"Yeah," Josh agreed.

They drank more of the dark, enticing liqueur, unaware of the heavy alcohol content concealed in the sweetened flavor.

Josh smiled. He had never realized what a nice guy Dudley was. Real quality under all the blubber.

"Quality," Josh said.

"Huh?"

"Quality." With a happy start of surprise he realized he hadn't stuttered on the difficult word. "Quality," he repeated.

"Yeah," said Dudley. He looked at his watch. "Oh, rats, we missed New Year's Eve." He got up, looked down at the pool. The revelers were standing in a circle singing, arms around each other's shoulders.

Josh raised his glass. "Happy New Year anyway."

"Okay, happy New Year anyway," Dudley said.

They stood watching the singing circle at the pool.

"That's my sister, the one with the big boobs."

Josh couldn't see anyone of that description but he didn't want to seem unappreciative. "Yeah," he said, hoping the monosyllable would cover the situation.

They sat down facing each other, smiling.

"How do you feel?" Dudley asked.

Josh thought a moment. "Dee . . . detached."

"De who?"

Josh laughed. "Tached. Fuh . . . floaty."

Dudley laughed. "Floaty McGoaty."

Josh laughed. This Dudley really had a hidden sense of humor. A real solid guy. He looked at Dudley. Well, not solid, kind of jelly, but good solid jelly. He laughed again.

"Good . . . suh . . . solid jelly."

"Jelly McBelly," Dudley came back.

They roared with laughter. What a pair, Josh and Dudley: the comedy kids.

Dudley poured another.

"Hey," said Josh, "we could get stinko."

"Stinko McGinko," Dudley said, slapping his thighs wildly.

They chuckled and sipped and laughed, feeling absolutely marvelous.

"Hey," said Dudley, "let's go downstairs, join the party."

"Uh-uh," Josh chuckled. "I'm nuh . . . not dressed."

Dudley laughed, got up, looked down at the pool. "Wow!" he said.

"What?"

"They're not either."

"Not what?"

"Not dressed. They're skinny-dipping!"

Josh got up, went to the window in time to see a beautiful female body, totally unclothed, standing on the diving board. Then shouts from the swimmers and she went in.

"Oh," Dudley said, "did you see that!"

The floodlights had been turned out around the pool, but the underwater lights caught the lovely diver as she swam underwater to the shallow end, where a splashing, laughing mass of young bodies was greeting the new year.

Dudley took off his sweater. "Come on," he said.

"Huh?"

"We're going skinny-dipping." He tried to step out of his pants and fell to the floor with a heavy thud.

Josh laughed. Dudley laughed, struggled to his feet.

"You chicken?" Dudley asked.

"Who's chicken?"

"Chicken McGicken," Dudley giggled.

Josh laughed, downed the rest of his drink. He pulled his sweater over his head. His arms wouldn't work right; he struggled with the sweater, muffling his head. "Hey . . . I'm lost."

Dudley struggled to his feet, pulled Josh out of his sweater. They stood in the middle of the room swaying, chuckling. The decanter was empty.

"Josh . . ."

"Yeah, Dudley."

"We're drunk, ol' buddy."

"No, you're drunk."

"No, I'm Dudley."

They roared.

"I'm Dudley," Dudley repeated.

It was a vast, cosmic joke; they couldn't stop laughing. They held onto each other swaying, patting each other's shoulders.

"You Josh . . ."

"No, I'm drunk."

The joke could go on forever but there was a party down there in the swimming pool, and what it needed was two fabulous stand-up comics.

They struggled with shoelaces, belts, zippers, buttons, and finally they were ready. Dudley stumbled toward the door.

"Wait," said Josh. He ran unsteadily into the bathroom and got himself a towel, draped it around his waist.

They stumbled down the stairs and fell in a heap of laughter at the bottom.

"Shh . . ." said Dudley. "We've got to sneak in."

"Suh . . . sneakin' Muh . . . Muh Geekin," Josh came back.

They dissolved in uncontrollable laughter, slapping each other on the bare shoulders. Finally, they struggled to their feet. Dudley, looking like a fat cupid, led the way into the darkened living room. They stopped at the open sliding door.

"Hey, you can't skinny-dip with a towel on."

Josh took off the towel but held it protectingly in front of him.

They slipped out onto the slate decking of the pool, both holding back a little, subduing their laughter. Dudley sidled toward the diving board.

Suddenly the flood lights went on.

Shouts went up from the shallow end of the pool. "Hey, turn it off! No lights!"

Then a plump female figure came running out of the dining room door. Josh didn't need to be told that this was Dudley's sister. They were impressive boobs all right.

"Get out! Get out!" the plump figure was yelling. "My folks are back!" She ran back into the dining room.

"Oh, no!" Dudley moaned.

"Whu . . . what is it?" Josh asked hazily.

"My folks. They do this. They go someplace, then they fight, so she says let's go home so they can fight at home."

Dudley took Josh by the hand. "You better get out of here; my old man does crazy things when they're fighting. He could call the cops and throw them all in jail for trespassing."

The skinny-dippers were piling out of the pool, running for their clothes.

"Whu . . . wait," Josh cried, "I've got to get dressed!"

"You've got to get out," said Dudley. "Come on."

Dudley pulled Josh around to the far side of the pool.

114

A gate opened into a small garden between the pool and the parking area. They crossed the garden, stumbling into the plants. Josh could see an angry man in the parking area yanking suitcases out of a car trunk.

"Ohhh, he's boiling," said Dudley. "Wait till he goes."

They hid in a clump of faded roses.

"Ouch . . ."

"Shut up!" Dudley hissed.

The angry man stormed into the house.

"Run!" Dudley whispered.

By now Josh's head was spinning in wild confusion. The alcohol was in charge.

Dudley opened the gate, shoved Josh through it.

Josh ran across the parking area, down the driveway, and out into the road. There were no sidewalks in this canyon, just one inhospitable nonconcealing road. Josh took off in a stumbling run, swinging his towel wildly. The lights of a car came around a bend. There was no place to hide. Josh kept running.

The car came on, slowed. "Hey," called a young, laughing voice. "Do you know that's indecent exposure?"

There was a burst of wild mirth from the car.

Josh pounded on, the car passed.

In the following darkness, Josh stopped for breath, his hands on his knees, gasping. He felt dizzy and a little sick. He straightened up, draped the towel around his middle, and began an erratic jog down the road. He couldn't penetrate the mystery of his feet, which seemed a long way from his head, and determined on a course of their own.

He knew vaguely where he was and that it was better going downhill than up. But he hadn't thought about dogs. Or a dog. He could hear it behind him panting rhythmically, its toenails clicking on the surface of the road. It sounded big. He turned his head. It was big. A gray-and-white monster running silently behind him.

"Go home!" Josh yelled.

The dog was in no mood to go home.

Josh slowed his pace, the dog slowed. Josh stopped, turned dizzily to face the dog.

"Go home," he said uncertainly. "Puh . . . please?"

The dog sat on his haunches, his tongue lolling, then got up, moved closer.

Alcohol works in mysterious ways; Josh had more sense than to take off his towel and snap it at the dog. But that's what the alcohol did, snapped the towel at the dog. And the dog grabbed the towel, shook it like a captured rat. And the dog, with the towel in his mouth, turned and ran back into the shadows he had come from.

"Hey!" Josh yelled.

Dog and towel were gone. Josh stood there swaying. He felt so awful, so naked, so abandoned. He stumbled to the edge of the road, sat on the curb. And threw up.

It might have been a minute, it might have been an hour later. Time disappeared. Then there was a pair of headlights coming down the road. Josh couldn't move. He felt too awful.

He heard the car stop, a door open and close. The beam of a flashlight caught him. He looked up into the blinding light.

He heard a gasp of surprise, then a chuckle. "Joshua ... Josh Taylor, what are you doing sitting there naked?"

The beam of the flashlight lowered. Through his liquorish haze, Josh saw the uniform, then the friendly face of Nick, the private security guard.

"M'okay," Josh mumbled. He struggled to his feet, opened the door of the car and flopped into the front seat. "Plu ... please ... huh ... home?" he said groggily.

Nick shook his head sadly. Today's kids were so full of awful surprises. He sighed, started the car and drove down the canyon.

The patrol car pulled into Josh's driveway. Josh struggled to sit up. "Thu ... thanks," he said thickly. Unsteadily, he got out of the car, walked a few feet, and fell flat on his face.

Nick got out quickly. He helped Josh up gently and half-carried, half-dragged him in his arms to the door and rang the bell. The sound of music and laughter came from inside the house.

116

The front door opened.

"Josh!" Sandra cried.

"It's okay, Mrs. Taylor," Nick said. "The kid's a little drunk, that's all."

Sandra looked apprehensively at the revelers in the living room. "Bring him in, please."

Josh opened one eye and saw his mother. The bottom fell out of the world. He closed the eye, surrendered to disaster.

There was no way you could sneak a sixteen-year-old skinny-dipper into the house unobserved. After the first cries of alarm at the limp body, there was unrestrained laughter as the revelers followed Nick down the hall to Josh's room. Sandra closed the door, and Nick laid Josh on the bunk. Sandra thanked Nick, let him out, and finally shut the door against the delighted hoots of the guests.

She looked at Josh sadly, pulled the cover over him.

Josh rolled on his back and opened his eyes, looking at the ceiling. "Chu . . . chicken . . . muh . . . MuhGicken," he said solemnly and passed out.

Josh didn't remember much about New Year's Eve, but his mother filled him in on his inglorious return home.

"Drunk and with no clothes on," said Sandra coldly. "Where are your clothes, Joshua?"

He couldn't speak. If he opened his mouth he'd be sick again.

"Joshua . . ."

He looked at her in panic, threw off the blankets and ran for the bathroom. She could hear him being very sick. She sighed heavily, left the bedroom.

Josh climbed back into bed and clung to the sideboards. The bed seemed to be rocking, floating, riding an endless wave of nausea.

When finally the bed came to rest he lay there exhausted, trying to remember what had happened the night before, how he had ever come to this awful state. And as he groped for recall, a weird thing happened. He closed his eyes and right there in front of him was a

117

screen, like a movie screen, and every minute of the night before began to play itself out, like a very bad movie. The syrupy drinks from the decanter, the skinny-dippers, the return of the parents, the naked flight into the night. He could almost hear a clicking, like a home movie, as the awful events flickered on the screen of his mind. The film ended abruptly when the dog snatched the towel. Josh tried to run it back again, but the reel was over.

He thought he was going to be sick one last time but there wasn't anything left to be sick with. He gagged once more and lay still.

He was asleep when Carmela came in with coffee and a small glass of something thick and reddish on the tray.

He opened his eyes. Carmela held out the glass.

He shook his head.

She looked at him sternly and pushed the glass closer. He knew he'd have to take the stuff.

The first taste was terrible, and it burned a little on the way down, but when it hit it wasn't so bad. He made a protesting face but took another sip of the stuff.

"Carmela . . ."

"Yes?"

"I feel awful."

She put her hand on his forehead. "Good," she said.

"Good?"

She nodded to the glass. "Finish."

He took another sip.

"All."

He finished the rest and made another face. "I got drunk last night, Carmela. I didn't mean to."

"I know," she said.

He smiled wryly. "Thu . . . that's what they all say, huh?"

She nodded.

"Carmela . . ."

She waited.

He shrugged. "Nothing."

She continued to wait.

"Duh . . . did you ever want to chu . . . chuck the whole thing, Carmela? Take off, be your own person?"

118

Carmela thought a moment. "A veces, si." She sighed. He looked surprised.

"There are times," she said softly.

He realized suddenly that he never thought of Carmela as having any life not connected with him and Howie. He had never asked about how she lived or anything. And now he asked himself sharply, did he really care? He looked at her, seeming to see someone he'd never seen before and he knew that he did care. Very much.

"Carmela, my head hurts. Could you ruh . . . rub the back of my neck?"

She drew her chair closer to the bed. He lay on his stomach. Her strong hands rubbed his shoulder blades and the back of his neck and he could feel the wonderful tenderness of her hands comforting him.

When he woke the sun was gone. He'd slept the whole day. But his head was clear and he didn't feel sick. He rolled over and saw the shoes Howie had given him.

He ran till dark, erasing the entire film of New Year's Eve from his mind.

Chapter Fifteen

Night and early morning low clouds.

For days after school started again the nightly weather report on the eleven o'clock news had been the same. The happy, up-beat voice of the anchor man recited the daily violence and obituaries that passed for news, then announced the invariably dreary weather forcast: Night and early morning low clouds.

There was an unreal sameness to the news, the weather, the days. And Josh sank into the shroud of overcast, hardly noticing when one day ended and another began. It was as if he had never really gotten over Dudley's liquid candy and was living in a perpetual fuzzy hangover, the world around him strangely alien.

At first Josh tried to establish a connection to something, someone. He groped for something to hold onto. He longed to go to Sandra, talk to her, establish a link. Late one night, seeing a light from under the door of her study, he reached out to knock. Embarrassed at the shame he knew she must be feeling after his depraved exposure in front of all her friends, he drew back his hand and slinked off to his room. That was the least he could do, save her the reminder of the humiliation he had caused her.

On two or three different evenings he picked up the telephone to call Howie. But each time he slammed it down again. What good would it do? "How are you?" he'd say. "Fine," Howie would say. And then what? Nothing, that's what. Just the pain of separation all over again. Finally, he began to reject all thoughts of Howie. He retreated from memories, from hope. It was easier that way.

It took a lot more conscious effort to shutter the lens on mind-glimpses of Laurie. Laurie, smiling. Laurie, laughing. Laurie, disappearing. Disappearing.

Yes, it was better not to think, not to remember, not to talk. Just get through it, whatever he was going through, a day at a time, an hour at a time, a minute at a time. Alone. By himself.

It wasn't all that hard to do. People didn't exactly seek him out, include him in their lives. Sometimes, even at school when he was surrounded by other kids, he felt alone. Well, maybe not alone, but sort of invisible, and he wondered if he were like the tree that falls in the forest, unheard because there was no one to hear the sound of its fall. Not that he was going to fall or disappear or anything. But if he did, who would care? Who would even notice?

Sandra never mentioned the New Year's Eve incident again. She actually spoke very little to him at all. But he knew she was still angry. He had watched her give Bill the silent treatment plenty of times. Almost as if they had arranged it, each carefully avoided the other, Josh dreading a confrontation in which he'd be asked to explain the unexplainable, and Sandra more than willing to wait for an apology for his idiotic, childish prank.

He had given up his morning runs, dragged himself out of bed only after he heard his mother's car pull out of the driveway. Then he would shower, dress, go down to the kitchen and eat whatever cereal he happened to reach on the shelf.

Carmela had gone for her usual winter vacation to see her relatives in Mexico and Josh wrapped the gloom of the house around him, relieved of making any kind of contact with anyone.

Generally, his mother telephoned in the afternoon to say she was working late, getting the spring collection ready to show. And Josh made it a point to be in bed before she came home. When she looked in on him, he pretended to be asleep.

At school, Josh got to his classes just before the bell rang and was first to dash out when they were dismissed.

At lunchtime, he found a rarely used place at a table partially hidden by the fresh-fruit dispenser. One day, Dudley Weiner spotted him, peeked around the dispenser and shouted, "Chicken McGicken!" and laughed in a high-pitched, wild hyena voice. Josh just glared at him till Dudley wound down and waddled away, but he knew he'd have to find another secluded place to have lunch.

While other kids moaned and groaned at the boring review work in class before the flurries of finals, Josh—unable to concentrate anyway—found a kind of perverse satisfaction in the mindless, dull routine.

Even the therapy sessions settled into a monotonous series of exercises in which Mary spoke a phrase and Josh responded either by repeating the words indifferently or by a simple nod of his head to let her know he understood what was wanted but didn't feel like playing the game.

Mary Taubin herself was worried. At each session Josh seemed to drift further and further away from her. And she finally took action. She tried to reach him, touch him, with all the techniques she knew. She even invented a few new ones. If she couldn't break down the wall between them, she'd climb over it, tunnel under it, go around it. But no matter what she did, she got no reaction, no response. She tried reasoning with him; he seemed not to hear her. She joked, teased; he sustained an implacable silence. She taunted, baited him; he stared at her blankly.

She found herself wishing he'd fight her, defy her. Anything would be better than this strange, robotlike behavior. She'd never faced this kind of thing before. She felt frustrated, helpless, as if she were jogging on a treadmill, getting no place. There was no reaching him, touching him.

Mary pulled down the window shade, turned on the overhead light. She sat down at her desk, looked at Josh's expressionless face. "The big red cat was fat and sassy," she said.

"The big red cat was fat and sassy," Josh repeated staring into space.

"Come back, come back, wherever you are," Mary said.

"Come back, come back, wherever you are," Josh repeated.

"How'd you like a big fat kick in the head?" Mary said.

"How'd you like a big fat . . ."

"Go soak your head!" Mary interrupted angrily.

"Go soak your . . ." Josh looked at her. "What?"

Mary walked to the door, picking up her jacket from the back of the sofa as she went. She turned back to Josh. "I'm going out for coffee, want to come?"

"Nuh . . . no thanks," Josh said mildly.

She looked at him for a moment, then walked out and slammed the door hard behind her.

Josh sighed, sat in the chair until he heard the bell ring for the next class. Then he got up and walked slowly out of the room.

It was cold sitting on the hard seats looking down at the football field, but that's where Josh had brought his lunch. Nobody would be there, he could be alone, could think it out, be his own person.

Be your own person. What a pile of bull! He remembered saying to Carmela on New Year's Day, "Did you ever want to chuck the whole thing, take off, be your own person?" How could you be your own person when you were only half a person, barely able to talk without sounding like a string of firecrackers? And what was your own person? What it was, really, was the person you wanted to be, not what you were. That fantasy person, that smooth-talking, easy-going jock. That man in charge, the one who made things happen, the one they smiled at. Come off it, Josh. That's a crock!

Yeah, a real pile of it. The trouble is you are trapped by your own anatomy. Vocal cords that do tricks, windpipe that gets away from you. And all this therapy garbage. Useless. You're stuck with yourself, and that's the size of it.

Josh finished the hot drink and capped his thermos. Stiff from the cold, he got up and worked his way down the seats.

"Hey you, Josh Taylor!"

He saw the track coach coming out of the aisle tunnel with three of his sprinters.

"Where you been, Josh?"

"Sick," Josh answered lamely.

The coach nodded to the sprinters to start warming up. He came over, smiled.

"You dropping us, Josh?"

"Nuh . . . no, sir," said Josh. He hadn't meant to say that. He wanted to say, "Yeah, I'm not interested anymore. I'm through."

"We're doing time trials Tuesdays and Fridays. I'd like to see you out there."

"Oh . . . okay, I'll buh . . . be there," said Josh.

Now why had he said that? He wasn't interested. It was just more and more bull.

But on Friday he was in the locker room putting on his new shoes.

"Where you been, man?" It was Eddie Lenz looking at him with a phony grin.

"Around," said Josh.

"Lisa was asking about you. How was that ski resort? Meet any sexpots?"

Josh shrugged. What he wanted to say was, "Why don't you go shove it!" But he knew he'd blow it on the word *shove*.

Eddie mimicked Josh's shrug and moved on.

The whistle blew to hustle them out of the locker room. In minutes they were running down the hill to the beach.

It was gray, cold, and a fog was building up out on the ocean. Josh ran with the pack, not concentrating on his pace as he usually did, not working out his moves. His mind was on Laurie. He saw her face. He felt the moment when they had kissed on the sleigh ride. Then, not noticing that the pack had moved ahead of him, he felt an awful, total, stomach-turning sense of loss. He had felt he'd never see her again but now he was certain

124

of it. Out of nowhere, this gray, foggy desolation, this void of utter loneliness.

On the first hill he became aware of his position. Last. Forty yards behind the pack. He picked up his pace mechanically, his body taking over the run.

But he wasn't with it. He was in the pack but not one of them. He could get inside their heads, knew how they were working out their moves, plotting their small strategies, urging their tired legs to cross the finish with the favored dozen who would be on the squad next spring.

At the turn on Fourth Street, the halfway mark, the beginning of the run back, Josh dropped out of the pack and stood on the curb till they had all passed. Some glanced back. One, a friend, waved for him to come on. Josh just stood there. And Eddie Lenz, who had seen him drop out, smiled.

Josh sat down on the curb. Not to catch his breath; he wasn't even breathing hard. He just sat down and thought, Stuff it. It wasn't worth doing. There was nothing at the end of the road, nothing worth having.

He sat there for a long time. Then he got up and began walking slowly toward home. He didn't notice that the fog had climbed up from the water, forcing the cars to put on their lights. One almost hit him as he crossed Sunset. The angry horn made him jump, but the car was gone before he could make a gesture of defiance.

He had to look at a lamppost sign to see that he was in his own canyon. As he walked slowly up the hill the fog thinned a little. He heard a puffing sound behind him and a kid on a bike passed him, straining up the hill. The kid said hi and Josh said hi and the kid vanished into the gray mist.

There was something about the way the kid fought the hill that reminded him of Howie. Feisty, determined.

He missed Howie. Very much. He could talk to Howie. Or just be in the same room with him. Or read to Howie, not stumbling on a single word. Or just go down to the beach and horse around. Like brothers. Brothers.

He got home and Carmela made him take a hot

shower. He hadn't been aware that he was shivering as he came in the kitchen door.

After the shower he sat in front of the TV for the rest of the afternoon, just barely aware of the motion on the screen, not taking in the story, just letting the TV numb him, stop him from thinking.

The next day he said he was feeling lousy. His mother was worried and departed late for her office. She had left him in the living room in his robe, looking at TV. When she came home, he was still there, asleep in the big chair, the TV still going.

His mother conferred with Carmela. They took his temperature. It was normal. They asked him how he felt. He said okay. But the next morning he still didn't want to go to school. His mother took him anyway.

He came home and sat in front of the TV.

"Haven't you got any homework, Josh?"

"Yeah," he said.

"When are you going to do it?"

"Later."

And it went that way for almost a week. His mother would drop him off at school and find him in front of the TV when she came back.

Even Carmela couldn't get to him.

His mother disconnected the TV. Josh retreated to his room and played the two records he had left, played them over and over.

His mother was worried enough to think about getting help. Help, in canyon talk, meant a psychiatrist, a shrink. Josh cut that one off fast. He took his bike to school, checked in every day, and disappeared to the beach. Mary Taubin was worried when he didn't show for two sessions. She called him at home.

Sandra finally talked it over with Jack Bender. Jack said it was just a kid phase and would pass, but Sandra said maybe Josh needed a man to talk to.

So they worked out a move that would look casual. Josh had always been interested in Jack's Bentley. The car was thirty years old and looked as if it had just come out of the showroom. Even in Beverly Hills, young males would linger to give it a look as it stood at the

126

curb. It was unique, classic, the last of the handsome convertibles.

Jack met Josh after school one day and said he had a business courtesy call on a client in Malibu. Would Josh like to come along? Josh shrugged.

"You can drive," Jack said. "Top down and all."

Josh couldn't resist.

Jack hadn't wanted to risk his Bentley to a kid driver but Sandra said they had to take a chance. Besides, Josh was a very good driver.

And he was. And the day was perfect. And the top was down.

They didn't talk at all on the way there. Jack seemingly couldn't find the right opening and Josh was too entranced with the car.

It was fifteen miles to Malibu, twenty minutes of pure pleasure for Josh. He waited in the car while Jack talked with the client.

They started back.

"Josh . . ."

"Yeah?"

"What's the matter with you?"

"Huh?"

Jack paused, as though realizing he was a little abrupt. "I mean, what's been eating you these last couple of weeks? Your mother's worried sick."

"Nuh . . . nothing's the matter."

"Nothing?"

Josh shook his head.

"You sit on the seat of your pants most of the day, you ditch school, you clam up when anyone tries to talk to you. That's nothing?"

Josh looked straight ahead at the road.

Jack lit a cigarette, leaned back in the seat, looked up at the cloudless sky. He smiled. "I used to be moody when I was a kid, I know how it feels. Is it a girl, maybe? Somebody you got in trouble?" He laughed to show that they were grown men and could talk of such things.

Josh's grip tightened on the wheel, he shook his head.

"Then what? You can tell me. It won't go any farther than this car."

Josh concentrated on the road. Jack smoked his cigarette, perhaps realizing he wasn't getting anywhere, that maybe a little tougher angle would work.

"Look, Josh, you're making it rough for everybody. Why not let us help you?"

"I duh . . . don't need any help."

"You do, Josh! You're moping around like a whipped pup. If something's eating you for the love'a Mike come out with it. We'll understand."

Josh glanced at Jack. "Whu . . . would you?"

"You bet we would. Listen, boy, some day I may be your father, and I'm not the kind that'll sit still for too much nonsense. Understand?"

Josh's heart started pounding. It was out now. What he had feared most of all, what had been at the back of his mind, the unspeakable, hideous possibility: Jack Bender, his stepfather.

"Josh! Look out!" Jack screamed as Josh let the car drift into the opposite lane. Jack grabbed the wheel, Josh recovered and pulled back into his lane and then onto the shoulder. He stopped the car, jumped out, and started running.

"Hey, come back here!" Jack yelled.

Jack got in the driver's seat, started after Josh. But Josh ran down a flight of stairs to the beach, darted around a food stand, and disappeared.

Jack stopped the car. Stupid, stubborn, crummy little kid! Who cared where he went!

Jack stomped on the accelerator. The Bentley shot out into traffic and down the highway.

Chapter Sixteen

Josh ran along the beach for three miles, then turned and started up the hill. He didn't ask himself why he was running in the direction of the school. He couldn't have explained why he burst into Mary Taubin's office during her after-school session with another student. He was almost as surprised as Mary to find himself inside her room; he was wild-eyed, gasping for air, his hair tangled damply around his face.

Mary looked at him, drew a quick intake of breath. "I'll see you next week, Susan," she said to the student seated before her desk. "Same time, okay?"

The student nodded, passed Josh without looking up at him, closed the door behind her.

Mary went to Josh, led him to the sofa, sat down beside him.

"I . . . I . . . he . . . he . . . he . . . suh . . . suh . . . said . . . wuh . . . wuh . . ." The words were blocked behind his lips, jammed one behind the other. His mouth was full of unuttered words pushing to get out, choking, strangling him. He could feel perspiration trickling down his forehead.

Mary took his hand. "It's okay, Josh. It's okay. Take your time, catch your breath."

But Josh couldn't wait. He had to tell her. He had to tell her what Jack had said. That stuff about when Jack became his stepfather. He had to tell her now. Inside his head, sentences tumbled, banged against each other, screamed for release. His face grew red, the cords in his neck swelled with his effort. "He cuh . . . cuh . . . can't . . ." but the words only smacked up against the ones that came before. They were trapped, impacted behind thick layers of swollen, unspoken syllables. He was confused, frightened. Why couldn't he speak? Why couldn't he get a word out?

"I know you're upset," Mary said. "Something went wrong. But you can speak. You can do it. You can do it, Josh."

He sucked air, but he could only hear the rasping sound of his breath. He felt his lips form the *you* sound but he couldn't hear it. He saw himself, like a goldfish, his mouth pursed in a small tight circle, unable to utter a word.

"It's all right. Take it easy." She patted his hand. "You can say it."

He withdrew his hand, leaned his head back against the sofa, closed his eyes against the tears burning behind his lids.

To Josh, Mary's voice sounded impersonal, cold. "Think, Josh. Think it out. You know how to do it."

Why couldn't she understand? Couldn't she see how stuck he was? "Cuh ... cuh ... can't," he blurted.

"You can," she said firmly. "You can. All the things you learned. They work if you work them. Try, please try."

Josh shook his head, the tears forcing themselves out, sliding down his cheeks. He clenched his fists, held his breath.

"No matter what happened, whatever it is, you can talk."

Josh stood up, glared down at her. She didn't understand. Or maybe she didn't want to. Maybe it was just as he suspected all along. Her stupid therapy, this mumbo-jumbo she was shoving on him didn't work. Couldn't she see that he couldn't talk? Why couldn't she see it?

Mary stood up and looked into his eyes. "You know what to do. You have all the tools. Use them."

He made one last effort. "Huh ... huh ... help me."

Her eyes never left his face. "You have to help yourself, Josh. You know how."

He started to turn away but she held his arm. Her voice softened. "Josh, we've gone over it all before. It doesn't matter what happens, good or bad. Whatever the problem is, whatever the crisis, it does not have to affect your speech. Unless you allow it. *You* have control."

He felt a sudden rage. He wanted to look away. He saw her as smug, self-satisfied, egotistical. He shook his head. He wouldn't let her giant ego force him to give what he couldn't deliver.

"You're copping out!" Mary said fiercely.

He shook her hand off his arm. He felt betrayed, abandoned. She was nothing but a phony, a shallow phony!

Her eyes glittered angrily. "You have a choice. It's up to you."

It took all his effort. His arms flailed, his body trembled. But he got it out. "Yuh . . . you . . . fuh . . . fuh . . . you phony!"

The operative word was *split*. The word kept bouncing around in his head, occupying all the space. Split. Get away. Chuck it. That's what he had to do. There wasn't any choice.

He walked almost blindly, unaware of anything going on around him. Across Sunset against the light, an angry horn, but he didn't hear it; all he heard was one word.

Split. Get out. Get away. Don't take any more of it; just go. He started up the canyon. But where to? Where would he go?

He knew the answer long before he asked himself the question. The answer must have been lying there a long time waiting for this final provocation. So where to? Where else? Who else? Howie, of course. His brother.

Jack Bender's car was standing in the driveway. He stood looking at the car, trembling. Was it anger? Rage at Jack Bender? Or was it this sudden, crazy idea? He felt choked up with excitement, with the wild, insane logic of the whole thing.

There it was, the way to go, the split. The hateful symbol of Jack Bender. Break with them all! Jack, Mary Taubin, his mother, all of them!

Josh looked in the window at the steering column. The key was in the ignition. He looked toward the house. He opened the door on the driver's side, got in. They might hear him start it so he took the shift lever out of gear. The car rolled slightly; he touched the brake, then let it roll again.

The Bentley eased quietly out of the driveway and down the hill. After the first turn, Josh stopped and turned the ignition key. The engine came to life with a quiet purr. Then Josh's heart beat loudly as the gas gauge needle turned to "full." Oh, good ol' Jack Bender had filled his tank! Goodbye you cheap, second-rate, no-good flake. So long, Jack Bender. Thanks for the use of the car.

Josh turned into Sunset heading east toward the Freeway. He had been to Skytop several times by car. It was simple. Route 14, then 395 all the way. A breeze. Three hundred miles. Bill had always made it in an easy drive. . . .

But Josh, what are you doing, man? You're stealing a car! That Bender creep will scream bloody murder, call the cops when he finds his car gone. Turn back, say you just wanted a little joy ride. Come on, come on, use your head, this isn't going to work. They'll nab you for sure.

The sign for the San Diego Freeway was just ahead. Josh, use your head; where is this going to get you? Where? Skytop, that's where. With Howie and Bill, that's where. You're going home, man. To your brother, Howie.

The Bentley turned right into the northbound access lane and entered the stream of traffic on the San Diego Freeway.

Josh didn't know how long he had been driving. There was no joy in the feel of the wheel, in the response of the engine; no sense of release or call of the open road or any of that bull. He was driving a vehicle, that's all, an escape tool; he was running away, splitting. How many times had he heard some kid say, "I'm going to split." Just talk. But now it was real. Now he was doing it. There was no return ticket.

The day was beginning to fade. He had gone through the desert and now the freeway had ended in a wide blacktop, but the sign assured him he was on the right road.

He tried to come down off the painful tension, but angry, violent thoughts kept racing around in his head. He had to check his speed again and again as the anger flowed into the throttle sending the needle up and over the limit.

Slow, slow, take it easy, man. Suppose that car behind is a cop. Okay, okay, keep it at fifty-five, let him pass. An unmarked car coming alongside! Oh, no, it is a cop! All right, let him look, just keep your hands steady. Don't slow down, that looks phony. Fifty-five, keep it steady, let him pass. Okay, okay, you stupid cop, go on, pass.

The cop passed and moved away rapidly. Josh took one sweaty hand off the wheel, put the back of it against his mouth, afraid he might let go his lunch.

The moment passed. He held onto the wheel but his foot was trembling on the throttle. He took deep breaths, forcing the calm, forcing himself to think. He remembered the town of Mojave from a previous trip and knew he'd gone about a hundred miles. He could make Skytop about eight or nine o'clock. Good. Then what?

Yeah. Then what? He'd be with Howie and Bill. The rest would take care of itself.

But he knew it wouldn't. This whole thing wasn't going to work. Why not just ram the car against that brick wall over there, jam it down to the floor, one good solid hit? Ahh, why not a cup of coffee?

He stopped at a roadside place and ordered a black coffee. The guy behind the counter kept looking through the glass at the Bentley, its racing green shining brilliantly under the neon "Eat" sign.

"What is it?" the guy asked.

"Buh . . . Bentley," Josh answered.

"German?"

"Uh . . . English."

"English. Old, huh?"

Josh nodded.

"Never seen one of them before."

133

Josh felt uneasy. He shouldn't have stopped, made himself and the car conspicuous. He hurried with the coffee, put a quarter on the counter and got up.

The guy kept looking at the car. "Sure never seen one of them before," he said as Josh went out the door.

No, it wasn't going to work. He was going to get stopped, dragged back to Jack Bender and his mother, to a scornful Mary Taubin, to an empty, stupid, go-nowhere life in the canyon.

No way. No way would they get him back. He swung the car out of the parking lot and onto the highway. Lights were on now, the sun had gone. He felt a little better. No way would they get him back. He moved the speed up to sixty, risking a little. He could still see the outline of mountains on either side. In an hour or so he would be climbing. Skytop was seven thousand feet up on the eastern side of the great Sierra Range. Two hundred miles of mountains steadily upward.

He turned on the radio, half expecting to hear a news bulletin with himself as the lead item, but the button he pushed brought in music. He let the music stay.

Now it was dark. His headlights picked out the elevation signs. Twenty-four hundred feet, thirty-five hundred feet. At four thousand feet it began to snow lightly.

Josh had never driven in snow. The wet flakes clung to the windshield, resisting the push of the wipers, piling up on the sides, making the road a white-bordered tunnel.

It was exciting in a way. The swirl of the snowflakes increased the feeling of speed, of meeting an adversary that had been waiting to challenge the Bentley.

An hour later, the wet snow changed to small, hard-driving flakes. At five thousand feet, the wind took over, piling dangerous drifts along the side embankment.

He began to feel uneasy. No cars were passing, the surface of the road was gone, the line between the road and the passing fields no longer visible. The snow-depth markers were the only safe guide, outlining where the road used to be.

Then the first skid. He didn't know it was happening till he tried to straighten the wheel on a gentle curve.

The tail swung out and he hit the snowdrift with a solid thud, bringing the car to a stop.

For a moment he panicked. For some obscure reason he turned off the windshield wipers. In seconds there was a frightening blanket of white over the windshield. He turned the defroster to high and the fan sent a blast of heat to melt the snow, showing the way ahead as if through heavy tears. He turned the wipers on again and the vision cleared.

He touched the throttle, the wheels spun a little, the rear swayed, and the car was back on the road again, picking its way carefully along the trail of snow-depth markers.

There wasn't any time to think of the complex of troubles that had unleashed this wild journey of escape. The big point was to come out of it alive.

He concentrated every ounce of strength on the driving. The snowflakes came in gusts, lashing the wipers, hissing venomously against the windshield. At times everything was obscured in a curtain of white, then, clearing, the headlights picked out a curve, a looming hill, a stretch of road that wasn't there.

Josh lost track of time, no longer looking at the dashboard clock. He passed through small towns shuttered against the storm, afraid to stop, fearful of going ahead. Surely by now there must be an alarm out, surely they were looking for him. He drove on, hour after hour. Then there was a junction sign, "Skytop 85."

Maybe he was going to make it. He began the last climb toward the rugged mountains. On Baler Summit, at six thousand feet, the Bentley seemed to pause for breath, the carburetor fighting the thin air. Then an elevation sign told Josh he was going down a long grade. Without previous knowledge, he sensed the right move and dropped the gear lever into low. For a second the reduced speed made the car side-slip, but then it caught and held steady.

It seemed forever crawling down the long grade. At the bottom was a turn and a level stretch. As his headlights slowly came around the turn, he hit the brakes and slid to a stop.

There was a girl standing in the middle of the road waving one arm frantically, holding a baby in the other. Behind her Josh could see one rear wheel high on an embankment, the rest of the car invisible, buried head first in snow.

The girl ran toward the headlights and in a moment a man climbed up the embankment and ran after her, then ahead of her.

The man banged on the door of the passenger side. Josh leaned over and unlocked it.

Without a word to Josh the man pushed back the passenger seat. "Come on, come on," he yelled at the girl.

She clambered into the back seat and fell against the cushions with a loud exhale of relief.

The man, young, mid-twenties with a yellow beard and steel-rimmed glasses, slammed the door shut, grinned at Josh.

"Thanks," he said. He turned to the girl. "The kid all right?"

"I think so," she said. "I think he's hungry."

The man turned back to Josh. "I told her not to bring the kid. He'd just be in the way. How far you going?"

"Sku . . . Skytop," said Josh.

"Okay, that'll do." He looked at the clock on the dashboard. "I got to be in Reno by noon tomorrow." Then back to the girl. "I told you not to bring him." Then once more to Josh. "That's our car with the wheel sticking up. Stop and we'll pick up the bags."

Josh couldn't believe this. He sat immobile for a moment. He couldn't kick them out, but the whole thing was somehow unreal. He stopped alongside the visible wheel while the young man brought out his bags and a guitar and tossed them in the back seat.

Josh gestured to the wheel of the stranded car. "Duh . . . don't you want to get huh . . . help?"

"The heck with the car," the young man said. "It's hers and it isn't worth anything." He laughed. "You won't have to make any more payments, Allie."

The girl giggled. "I wasn't going to."

The young man held out his hand to Josh. "Name's Dan."

Josh held out his hand reluctantly. "Juh . . . Joshua."

"Glad to know you, Joshua. She's Alice. That's her kid, not mine." He checked the clock. "Hey, man, we better get going."

Josh moved ahead slowly. The snow had lessened but was still falling. He drove in silence, feeling uneasy, not knowing why.

Dan unbuttoned his parka, drew out a pack of cigarettes, held them out to Josh.

"No, thanks," Josh said.

Dan took the lighter out of the dash, lit his cigarette. As he put the lighter back he touched the dash admiringly. "Real wood, huh?"

Josh had never noticed. "Yeah," he said.

Dan leaned back in the seat, exhaled with obvious pleasure. Josh concentrated on the road. In the lower edge of the rear view mirror he could see the girl. She was breast-feeding the baby.

"Skytop," Dan said, looking ahead.

Josh nodded.

"Skiing?"

Josh shook his head.

"I skied once. Went flat on my can." He laughed. "This your car?"

"No. Fuh . . . friend of mine."

"Nice car," said Dan. He felt the seats. "Real leather, huh?"

"Yeah," said Josh.

"I'll bet a car like this could bring a lot of money in Reno. Who's that guy that's got a museum? I bet he'd give a nice chunk for a car like this." He looked at Josh, smiling. "Your friend's car, huh?"

Josh nodded.

"Hey, Allie, don't he look like Phil?"

Alice looked at the back of Josh's head. "Sorta."

"Phil got busted bringing stuff in from Mexico," Dan said. He smoked in silence for several minutes, lowered the window, and threw his cigarette out. He leaned his head back on the seat. "I sure do like this car."

Josh kept concentrating on the road. There was an occasional car coming on. Neither driver was sure of the edge of the road, so they met closely, headlights glaring blindingly against the snow.

"You know what I'd do if I had a car like this?" Dan said. "I'd go down to Baja, pick up a couple of kilos of coke, I'd dress up real fancy . . . for cryin' out loud, look out!"

The oncoming car was crowding Josh. He gripped the wheel desperately, the car passed, the Bentley slid into a shallow ditch and came to a stop.

"That crazy idiot!" Dan yelled. "He coulda killed us!" He turned to Josh. "Nice driving."

Josh didn't answer. All at once he was aware that he couldn't talk at all, that he could move his lips but the words weren't going to come out. The dread had always been there, hidden, that this would happen some day, that the words wouldn't come out at all.

"Try moving it out real slow," Dan said.

Josh looked at him blankly.

"Rock it easy. You can rock it out. Go ahead, try."

Josh hardly heard. His heart was pounding with fear. It was here, the final disaster. He couldn't talk.

"Go ahead," said Dan. "Try rocking out."

Mechanically, Josh touched the accelerator. The wheels spun hopelessly.

Dan got out of the car and went to the back. "Try again!" he yelled.

Josh touched the throttle; Dan pushed; the wheels spun.

Dan came to the driver's side. "You push, I'll get it out of here."

Stiffly, Josh got out of the car, slipped in the snow as he went to the back.

Dan sat in the driver's seat. With delicate foot he touched the throttle, moving the shift lever from drive to reverse. The car began to rock back and forth. Josh put his hands against the rear and gave a push. With a final lurch the car spun out of the ditch, swerved, ploughed into the center of the road.

Dan leaned out of the passenger window, grinned broadly at Josh, and waved. "So long, Joshua. Thanks for the lift!"

Chapter Seventeen

Josh, stumbling in the snow, ran wildly after the moving car. The Bentley jerked ahead, its exhaust spewing smoke, its rear fishtailing, swerving crazily. Then it gained speed and continued down the road. As he ran, Josh saw the taillights dance with the motion of the car, gobbling up distance.

His arms flailing, his feet plowing up clods of newly fallen snow, Josh chased the Bentley. He skidded, slid on the slippery road, then he gradually slowed his pace. There was no way he could catch up with the automobile. He stopped running. In less than thirty seconds the car turned around a bend and was gone.

His mind hollered, "Hey! What're you doing? Come back you dirty creep! Stop!" His lips moved, his mouth opened, but no words rushed out. Not a single utterance. Not one sound. Nothing. He stood there disbelieving, his tongue still working to shape the unspoken words. His lips stretched and contracted as if in spasm. In turn, his cheeks puffed out, pulled in. He could see his breath, little unformed shots of white clouds issuing into the freezing air. He struggled to release a word . . . any word. Nothing.

He pulled himself rigidly erect, brought his arms down stiffly against his sides and yelled from the bottom of his rage. A loud, hoarse, guttural scream erupted. Releasing animal-like, agonizing sounds, he bellowed, roared unintelligibly, giving voice to his hopelessness, his powerlessness; the harsh ragged outcries pronouncing his wordless, total surrender.

Then, panting, he sank to his knees on the icy pavement. He sat back heavily, looked around. There was no sound but the lightly falling snow and his own rasping breath. Thin light from the snow was enough for him to make out the road and the white, looming hills on either side.

He crawled to the shoulder of the road, slumped onto his side. He put his head on one arm, the snow falling on his hair, gathering on the thin windbreaker, his only cover.

And then he cried helplessly, without restraint, his shoulders heaving, hot tears mixing with the snow on his cheeks. He sobbed until he was exhausted, until, emptied of all feeling, his breath quieted. He was numb, beyond cold, beyond grief. He lay there, the snow piling up on his head, his shoulders, his hips.

Slowly, he became aware that he had to get up, get moving. But he didn't get up. He didn't move. He lay still.

Why not stay here? Sink into sleep. Let go, float, drift away. It would be so easy. He closed his eyes. He felt sleepy, drowsy, almost comfortable. Fragments of thoughts faded in and out of his mind. Sandra. His mother. So beautiful. He embarrassed her, was in her way, her responsibility. He lay motionless, thinking of himself. Dumb kid. Stupid jerk. The Bentley. He had let it get stolen. Jack Bender. Stepfather Bender . . .

The wind rose, snow drifting around Josh's legs. Still, he lay there. Car gone. Howie gone. Howie . . .

From way off somewhere, Josh heard a dog barking. Joshua. Josh. Hey, man, get hold of yourself. You're not far from Skytop, from your brother. Get up. Get going. Get moving.

He forced his eyelids open, got up on his knees, then struggled to his feet. Staggering, his feet slogging through the snow, he began to walk. In minutes his sneakers were soaked. His hands, thrust into the pockets of the jacket, were numb with cold. Unaware of the movement, he picked up his pace. Following the deep ruts in the snow made by the Bentley, he began to jog. It was something to fix on, the tire tracks of the Bentley. That was the way to go, head down, like a dog sniffing the trail. Keep your eyes on the tire tracks, Joshua.

It was unreal. Jogging, slipping, sliding, following the tracks that were filling with snow. He felt the cold now, wet, penetrating; the wind chilled him clear through.

Abruptly, the crossroad sign came up out of the total whiteness. It pointed to Reno in one direction, Skytop in the other. Skytop—four miles. The tire tracks went toward Reno.

Josh stopped, gulping large breaths of cold air. Then, hands jammed deep in his pockets, his hair, eyebrows, shoulders powdered with snow, he began the last four miles to Skytop.

It was only ten o'clock but the entire village of Skytop seemed to be asleep. There was no one around to notice Josh as he stumbled along Sky Lane toward the complex of condominiums with steep-pitched roofs sticking up through the cover of new snow.

Eleven-o-four Sky Lane Road. Josh kept repeating it over and over in his head. And there it was suddenly, the numbers glowing above the mailbox. He pushed open the gate. Warm yellow light was showing behind the curtains of the large window in the living room.

Josh stood on the doorstep, supporting himself with one hand against the wall. He pushed the bell, heard it ring inside, but nothing happened. He pushed it again.

The living room curtains opened a crack and Howie looked out, Josh could hear his yell through the thick doors and window.

"Josh!"

The door was flung open.

"Josh, Josh!"

Howie threw himself on Josh, grabbing him in a wild bear hug. Josh could barely stand, but he held onto Howie.

"Josh, how did you get here, are you here for good, where's Sandra, Bill's at a meeting, why didn't you call?" The questions rattled out wildly.

Howie released Josh, slammed the door shut, took a good look at him. "Man, you look terrible, like somebody dragged you through a car wash. What happened? How did you get here?"

The sudden warmth of the condo hit Josh like a blast of hot air. It nearly knocked him out. He wiped his nose with the back of his hand, tried to answer Howie. But his lips were still stiffened with cold. What came out was a feeble groan.

Howie looked at the wet sneakers, the melting snow already forming a little pool at Josh's feet. He noted the thin windbreaker. "You didn't walk here?"

Josh nodded weakly, then shook his head. He wanted to say, "Yes, I walked; no, I drove." He wanted to tell Howie everything, but what he heard issuing from his throat was a series of strange clacks. His teeth were chattering uncontrollably. He clenched his teeth together, took a deep breath, tried again. Panic seized him when he heard himself utter a stacatto of grunts. He put a hand over his mouth. Maybe if he had something hot to drink . . . he looked into the open kitchen.

"Coffee. You want coffee," Howie said.

Josh shuffled unsteadily to the stove, picked up the tea kettle. When he thawed out, he told himself, he'd be able to speak.

Howie followed him, took the kettle from his hand. "I'll do it. You sit down."

Josh smiled wanly, turned, and went into the living room. He flung off his wet windbreaker, dropped onto the leather sofa. Once more he attempted to say something. His mouth opened, closed. Again it opened and again it closed. He couldn't talk. He couldn't say anything. Was he mute? His stomach churned. Would he never be able to speak again? Had the worst of all his fears finally come to pass? Or was this some kind of weird nightmare?

Hold on. It would pass. Be cool, he told himself. It was the cold, the exposure, the stress. But was it? He leaned back against the sofa. Sure, once he had his coffee . . .

Howie was shaking as he lit the gas under the kettle. He kept looking at Josh, spilled the teaspoon of instant coffee as he dug it out of the container.

It scared him, the way Josh looked, the way he leaned

into the sofa as if he didn't realize where he was, as if he were in another world.

Howie could hardly believe it. Josh was here. He couldn't have walked all the way; he didn't come with Sandra. He must've split, hitchhiked, maybe. He must've cut out, but how did he ever . . . And why wouldn't he talk? Josh had never had any trouble talking to him before.

As the kettle came to a hissing boil, Howie saw Josh lie down, put his feet up on the sofa. Howie poured the water into the cup. Shakily he carried the cup into the living room, set it down on the low table in front of Josh.

Josh was asleep. Howie unlaced the wet sneakers. Josh stirred, moaned in his sleep. Howie pulled off the wet socks, went to the hall closet, got a blanket and threw it over his brother.

Josh raised his head, looked at Howie, and went back to sleep.

Howie sat there just looking at Josh. Then he heard the garage door open. He went into the kitchen as Bill came in. Howie put a forefinger to his lips, "Shhh," he whispered.

"Shhh what?" Bill answered.

Howie pointed to Josh on the living room sofa.

"What the . . . how did he . . ."

"I don't know. He can't talk."

"When did he . . ."

"Ten minutes ago. The bell rang and there he was."

Bill went into the living room. He knelt down beside Josh.

"He sure looks beat," Howie said softly.

Bill felt Josh's head. "How did he ever . . ."

Josh felt the hand pulling him back from sleep. He opened his eyes.

"Hi, Josh," said Bill softly.

Josh sat up.

Bill picked up the coffee, held it to Josh's lips. Josh took several large swallows.

"You all right?" Bill said, putting down the cup.

"Uh . . . uh . . . uh . . . uh . . ." Then, softly moaning, he put his hand up on Bill's shoulder.

"Josh," Bill soothed. "It's all right. You're tired, you need some sleep. You'll be fine in the morning."

Josh looked at him, shook his head.

"Believe me, you'll be okay. Come on, right now it's bed for you."

Bill and Howie helped Josh up the stairs to the spare bedroom. He flopped on the bed letting them pull off his shirt and soggy jeans. They covered him with a fat down quilt and turned out the light.

In the kitchen, Bill poured a drink for himself and a glass of milk for Howie. They sat at the kitchen table, and Bill said with a reluctant sigh, "I guess I'll have to call Sandra."

And Howie repeated the sigh and said, "I guess you will."

Chapter Eighteen

Howie fiddled with his breakfast cereal, looked up at Bill. "Do I have to go to school?"

"Yes."

"Why?"

"Because I said you have to go to school."

"That's a lousy reason."

Bill smiled, touched Howie's head affectionately. "Because I don't want you in my hair when I'm talking to Sandra."

"That's better," said Howie. He ate two more spoonfuls of cereal.

"She'll take him home, won't she?" Howie asked.

"Yes."

"Then why do I have to . . ."

"Howie, I promise you, I won't let her take Josh till you have a chance to say good-bye. You can come home after lunch."

"Okay," said Howie. He ate some more cereal. "She was pretty wound up on the phone, huh?"

"Yeah, she was very wound up."

"Did she say Josh stole Jack Bender's car?"

"That's what she said."

"And you told her Josh walked here, he didn't steal anything."

"Well, what I said . . ."

"Anyway, stealing a car from somebody like Jack Bender wouldn't be stealing."

"Howie."

"Yeah?"

"Finish your cereal and go to school."

"Okay. But you promise . . ."

"I promise. Josh will be here when you come back."

"Okay."

Howie finished his cereal, took a piece of toast, and stood up. "See you later."

Bill gestured with one arm. Howie came over for a good solid hug. "See you later," Bill said.

Howie left, chewing the piece of toast.

Bill heard the door close. He sighed heavily, stirred his coffee uselessly. Dealing with Sandra wasn't going to be pleasant. She had been almost hysterical when he got her on the phone and told her Josh was in Skytop. She had immediately accused him of arranging the whole thing and had demanded that Josh be brought to the phone. He told her Josh couldn't talk; Josh was in bed, exhausted. Well, where was the car? she had asked. He didn't come by car, Bill had answered. He walked. At that point it had gotten confused and heated. He said she was more concerned about a lousy car than her son and she had said she was now positive he had planned the whole thing. Then he had hung up.

She had called him back and said she was leaving as soon as it got light. Then she had hung up.

Bill figured she'd be in Skytop sometime before noon. The snow had stopped and the plows were out. He hoped she wouldn't bring the Bender jerk, Bill felt like he might just take a poke at the guy.

He called his office and said he wouldn't be in, then he turned on the TV to the financial station and looked at the stock quotes. He noticed that the oils were taking a beating and he was mildly pleased because he had advised several of his clients to go short on the oils and it was working out nicely.

The morning dragged. He went upstairs three times to check on Josh. The last time he stood holding the door open a little, looking down on Josh, he felt tender, protective, close. Emotions he hadn't known were there.

The front buzzer rang a little after twelve when Bill was in the kitchen making another pot of coffee. He went to the front door.

"Hi," Bill said. "Come on in."

Sandra came in without a greeting. Bill was pleased that Bender wasn't with her.

"How about a cup of coffee?" he asked.

She looked very tense, unyielding, but she managed a polite smile. "I think I need one."

She followed him into the kitchen. He put two fresh cups on the table.

"Where's Josh?" she asked.

"He's still asleep. I just checked."

"I'd like to start back as soon as possible, the roads are bad."

"Okay." He poured the coffee. "Sit down."

She took a sip of her steaming coffee, put down the cup. "What's this about Josh not talking?"

"Just that. Literally. He just doesn't seem to be able to speak at all."

"That's nonsense. He's just clamming up."

"I don't think so, Sandra. I think it's more serious."

"Yes, it's serious. He stole a car and ran away from home. That is very serious."

Bill shrugged. "Okay, say it your way."

"You don't think stealing a car is serious?"

"Sandra, the kid is just two jumps ahead of a nervous collapse. The car was just a prop, a breakaway tool. He's got more on his mind than just joy-riding."

"More of what?"

Bill took a deep breath. "Look, I want to say something and I want you to keep your mouth shut for two minutes."

"How do you dare . . ."

He grabbed her arm, held it very hard. "Shut up, Sandra."

She didn't move. He released her arm slowly.

"Those boys need each other . . ." he began.

"Not that again," she said irritably.

"They need each other," Bill said firmly. "We never should have separated them; we should have seen what it would do."

"Are you suggesting . . ."

"No, I'm not. I'm over that, over you and me. If you're interested, there might even be someone else . . ."

147

"I'm interested in my son and I'd like to get back to Los Angeles as soon as possible."

"Sandra, these kids are entitled to a life of their own. We were so involved in our own problems, we never considered them."

"You evidently solved yours," she said acidly.

He smiled. "Honey, I've got to confess, I'm growing up. Having Howie, taking on, heaven forbid, responsibility, I'm practically a grown man."

Sandra looked at her watch. "That's nice."

"One last pitch, Sandra. Let Josh stay. At least for a while till he works things out in his head."

"I'm sorry, Bill." She stood up.

Bill didn't get up. He nodded upward. "He's in the bedroom on the right at the top of the stairs."

Sandra climbed the stairs slowly. She was very tired, upset, drained by the tension of the last twenty-four hours, by the grief and shock when she found that Josh had gone. Then both the relief and anger that he had gone to Skytop. Just before she left home, Jack had called to tell her the Bentley had been recovered by the police. That helped, but it still didn't excuse Josh's behavior.

She couldn't take it all in, the suddenness of it. Josh had always been such an easy kid, had seemed to love her, to admire her. Then to have him abandon her, reject her, steal Jack's car and take off. It didn't make sense. She'd been a good mother, given him everything he'd ever needed, tried to be friends. Hadn't she taken him to Winter Valley, a wonderful time of skiing? Some mothers would have left the kid at home. What did he want?

She stopped at the top of the stairs, hesitated before the closed door. What did all the kids want these days? To run their parents' lives, tell mommy to come home at ten o'clock, and not have any friends? Male friends? They asked too much, far too much these days.

She opened the door, went into the room. Touched at once with tenderness and anger, she stood looking down at Josh. She crossed to the window, pulled up the slatted blinds. She sat in a chair next to the bed.

"Joshua," she said softly.

Josh stirred, rolled over.

She waited, then she shook him gently. "Joshua . . ."

He opened his eyes, stared at her.

"Joshua, darling, it's time to go home. Get up and get dressed, okay?"

Josh didn't move.

"The roads are bad, darling. We've got a long drive."

She got up, took his trousers off the footboard, tossed them playfully on the bed. "Let's go, son."

Josh sat up slowly. He looked at her. Not with anger, not with rebellion, but almost as if she were a stranger, someone he didn't know at all.

"We'll stop at a coffee shop in the village, have a big breakfast. I brought your ski jacket; it's in the car."

Josh sat there, staring at her. She looked like a model, her blonde hair glistening, her colorful jacket draped casually over her shoulders. The soft scent of her perfume hung in the air.

She nodded at the trousers lying on the covers. "It's getting late."

Slowly, Josh extended his hand, picked up the trousers. He waited.

"Move, Joshua," Sandra said with a slight hint of irritation in her voice.

Josh eased his legs off the bed, dragged the trousers over his lap, then looked at his mother.

She gave a short laugh, turned her back to Josh. "I'll wait while you dress."

His jeans had dried stiff. They made a crackling sound as Josh drew them up over his legs. He looked around the room, saw his T-shirt and socks draped over a chair. He put on his T-shirt, smoothed it down over his hips. He picked up one sock, then the other. Holding a sock in front of him as if he had forgotten what it was for, he sat down on the chair.

"Come on, slow motion," Sandra said over her shoulder.

Josh bent to put on his sock. He noticed every detail as he pulled it on, the tight ribbing, the blue fuzzy

149

stripe around the cuff, the paperlike feel of the usually soft fabric.

"Your shoes, Joshua. Over there," Sandra said from the doorway.

Josh looked at his shoes partly hidden under the bed. He padded toward them, picked them up, cradled them in his hands.

"Put them on. Put them on, Joshua," his mother said.

Josh sat down on the bed, began to put on his right sneaker.

"You'll feel better after you've had something to eat," Sandra said a little more gently. "We'll have steak and eggs and gallons of coffee and . . ."

They heard the bang of the front door slamming shut, then Howie's voice: "Where's Josh, that's Sandra's car in front, he's not leaving yet, is he? Hey, Josh . . . Josh . . ."

It was as if Josh had suddenly come awake. He was standing beside his mother at the top of the stairs. All this was real: Sandra here; Howie hurrying to the staircase; Josh leaving. It was real.

"Hello, Howie," Sandra said.

Howie nodded, his eyes on Josh. He was about to rush up the stairs when Bill came in, put his hands on Howie's shoulders, held him back.

"Come on, Joshua," Sandra said. "Say good-bye to Howie and Bill and we'll be on our way."

But Josh stood there taking it all in, looking down at Howie. Howie's eyes, staring at Josh, were pinpoints of blue in the very pale face.

Sandra started down a couple of steps, then stopped and looked back. "Coming?"

Josh knew what he wanted to say, what he needed to say. The words pronounced themselves clearly in his mind. But he also knew he couldn't talk. It would be a mistake to try. He could almost see the horror on her face if he came out with those freaky, weird sounds . . . those inhuman croakings.

She smiled up at him, waiting. He shook his head. The smile left her face; she looked at him questioningly.

He had to talk. He had to do it. His face muscles began to work, his fists clenched with the effort.

"What is it, Joshua?"

He thought quickly back to Mary Taubin, to that awful last session. "You can speak if you want to, you can do it."

And now he wanted to more than at any time he could remember. He wanted to speak; he had to speak. His body felt damp, clammy, as if his clothes hadn't fully dried. He sucked in deep breaths remembering Mary Taubin, the orange-colored paperback, the diagrams illustrating air-flow. But could he do it?

Josh looked down at Howie again. He saw Bill tighten his fingers over Howie's shoulders as the boy strained over the stairs, his eyes fixed on Josh, his lips parted.

"Well, Joshua?" Sandra said tightly.

"I . . ." He struggled. "I . . . I'm nuh . . . not going . . ."

Sandra came back up beside him, put her arm around his waist. She smiled thinly, looked at Bill. "I knew he could talk, just clamming up again." Then to Josh: "All right, let's go."

Josh faced her, looked directly at her. His breath labored, he jammed his hands into his pockets to hide the trembling. "I . . . I'm nuh . . . not going home."

She dropped her arm, stared at him with supressed rage. "Josh . . . I'm your mother!" she said as if it were an order.

"I . . . I . . . I'm stuh . . . staying huh . . . here with Howie."

He heard her quick intake of breath; for an instant he almost relented. He loved his mother.

"I won't let you! I'm taking you home. Where you belong!" Sandra said.

Josh's face was deadly pale. He spoke so quietly he could hardly be heard. "If . . . if you tuh . . . tuh . . . take me home, I'll ruh . . . ruh . . . run away . . . I'll come buh . . . back here. Fuh . . . first chance I guh . . . get, I'll cuh . . . come back."

Sandra looked down at Bill. Both Bill and Howie, their faces strained, remained silent. She turned back to Josh, looked at him bleakly.

Josh noticed an almost imperceptible slump of her

shoulders. He couldn't face the hurt he knew he was causing her.

"I . . . I'm suh . . . sorry, Mom, I'm suh . . . sorry. But I'm nuh . . . not going home."

She turned and ran quickly down the stairs. Then she stopped and looked up at him again as if she expected him to change his mind. Then Josh noticed tears well in her eyes before she turned to Bill: "I'm leaving him with you for the present. We'll talk on the phone."

She hurried to the entry, opened the door. Then Sandra closed the door and was gone.

The digital clock with the glaring red numbers told Josh it was 1 A.M. It told him he hadn't been asleep and wasn't going to go to sleep.

Those last moments with his mother had been rolling over and over in his mind since he'd gone to bed. He kept seeing the slump of her shoulders, the hurt on her face, her defeated expression when she had told Bill she'd be calling him. Josh kept hearing the slam of the door when she had left. The closing door had sounded so final.

Josh knew what was bothering him. Guilt. Crunching guilt. The guilt at the pain he had caused his mother. He felt suffocated by it, all but swallowed up in it. Bone-deep, stomach-churning guilt.

He rolled over on his side, his pajamas twisted around his legs. He'd never get to sleep, he thought, as he tried to shake his pajama legs free.

He heard a soft tapping at his open door, then Howie's subdued voice: "Josh, you asleep?"

"No."

"Me either."

Josh sat up, turned on the lamp.

Howie came over to the bed, sat on the end facing Josh, leaned against the footboard. There was a book tucked under his arm.

"Josh?"

"Yeah?"

"Wanna read?"

"Sure," Josh said. "Why not?"

152

Howie tossed Josh the book. It was the same one Josh had slipped into Howie's duffle bag before his brother left for Skytop. For some dumb reason or another Josh felt a catch in his throat.

"The corner's turned down," Howie said. "Where I left off."

Josh flipped through the pages, found the turned down corner. From the condition of the pages, he knew Howie must have read the book through several times.

Josh began to read: "'. . . and then the whirling ball of fire hurtled toward the helpless spacecraft. In seconds the world could come to an end, the universe could shatter . . .'"

Josh read clearly, faultlessly, with no trace of a stammer, spinning out the sentences in an even, relaxed, smoothness. He stopped to turn a page.

"Go on. Keep reading," Howie murmured sleepily.

Josh read on. He read page after page to the end of the chapter and then the book was finished.

He looked up. Howie was asleep, his head cocked crazily on the edge of the headboard.

Josh put the book on the nightstand. He took his extra pillow and gently laid Howie's head on it.

Then he went back to his own side of the bed and turned out the light. He dropped his head into his pillow.

He knew now he could sleep.

ANNE SNYDER, in addition to writing books and educational material, is active in the field of television. She is also a teacher of creative writing, and has taught at Valley College, Pierce College and University of California, Northridge. Her novel, *First Step*, published by Signet in paperback, was a winner of the Friends of American Writers Award, and became an ABC-TV Afternoon Special. *My Name Is Davy—I'm an Alcoholic; Goodbye, Paper Doll*, and *Counter Play* are also published by Signet. She and her husband live in Woodland Hills, California.

LOUIS PELLETIER, co-author of *Two Point Zero*, as well as *Counter Play*, includes among his many TV credits such shows as *General Electric Theater, Hawaiian Eye* and *The Love Boat*. Long associated with Walt Disney Studios, he scripted such movies as *Big Red, Those Calloways*, and *The Horse in the Grey Flannel Suit*. A resident of Pacific Palisades, Pelletier has taught screenwriting at University of California, Northridge, and U.C., Riverside.